VIKTOR

RED BRATVA BILLIONAIRES

COCO MILLER

COCO MILLER ROMANCE

Want to be notified when I release my next book or give away freebies?

JOIN MY LIST

Copyright © 2019 Coco Miller
All rights reserved.

Coco On Facebook
Coco On Instagram
www.CocoMillerRomance.com

LICENSE NOTE

This book is a work of fiction. Any similarity to real events, people, or places is entirely coincidental. All rights reserved. This book may not be reproduced or distributed in any format without the permission of the author, except in the case of brief quotations used for review.

This book contains mature content, including graphic sex. Please do not continue reading if you are under the age of 18 or if this type of content is disturbing to you.

BOOKS BY COCO

Big City Billionaires
Faking For Mr. Pope
Virgin Escort For Mr. Vaughn
Pretending for Mr. Parker

Red Bratva Billionaires
MAXIM
SERGEI
VIKTOR

INTRODUCTION

Warning: this love story isn't for the faint of heart.

Her little sister is underaged and looking for a job.

He's a Russian mafia boss who runs a strip club.

And hires her by mistake.

They may be tight on money.

But big sis' isn't haven't it.

She storms angrily in the club to take the mobster to task.

And sparks pop off like popcorn.

Then he makes her an offer she can't refuse.

And now she's in deep.

It's all kind of crazy.

VIKTOR is a steamy, workplace romance, stand-alone, Russian mafia romance. It is not appropriate for readers under 18 due to sizzling HAWT love scenes!

PROLOGUE

KENNEDY

THEY SAY FALLING in love is easy, as easy as riding a bike. Well sometimes riding a bike is difficult. Your feet can get stuck in the spokes or you could wobble and fall off of it. So I don't know if I believe ...them.

I think falling in love is more like breathing. Our hearts are built to open up, built to let another inside, to absorb another's pain, to learn, grow, feel, and sometimes... they break.

Love is a gift. Holding someone's heart should be cherished not taken advantage of. Sometimes you can't help who you fall for. Sometimes you fight the feeling, wishing it away, not wanting to fall at all.

I was in no place in my life to fall for any silliness. I had my sister to protect. I had dreams to achieve. I feel though that sometimes life doesn't care what you have planned. Like it's life's mean little trick to throw you off guard and blindside you.

Life is messy. It's hard and long and it takes everything you have to get through it for most of us. And for what? The hardest part of life is living itself, and God knows that I know this more than anyone else. I was given a crash course of a hard life. It has been hard since the day I lost both of my parents. The day I swore to the heavens above that I would take care of my sister in their place no matter what. At first it wasn't too bad, but then she turned into this unruly teenager that made me want to pull my hair out...and hers.

Yet putting all that aside, I felt I could do it. I felt I could trudge through life and make it. I was optimistic in a pessimistic situation. I was more than ready to rock my life out, on my own, and for my sister. Make the best of it. But I should have known things aren't always that easy. I should have known that meeting a bad man was probably in the cards for me. That falling for a bad boy was inevitable.

I had always been fine being alone. I didn't need a man to help me or take care of me. Fuck that. I am a strong, beautiful, woman who could handle anything this life threw at me, and a man would never be the answer to all of my problems.

Or would he?

CHAPTER ONE

KENNEDY

DO you know what it is? It's just a hyped-up mess. That's it. Life isn't that damn great. Sure people hype it up to be this amazing thing. People always talking about keeping a gratitude journal, counting your blessings and all that Oprah jazz; but for those of us who can't see past the grey skies and bleak horizon, what blessings?

I haven't always been this hopeless, this depressed, this down-on-life, woe is me type of girl. No, I once had dreams. I once had goals. I once thought life would be amazing too. That was a long time ago though, because now all I see is despair, especially when it comes to my little sister Terrica.

I take care of her, or at least I try to, but as soon as she hit her teens, Terrica stopped listening to me. Which is really hard considering that we're broke. I work every day trying to keep the lights on and the bills paid and it's not easy. Terrica offered to get a job, but I would rather her focus on her studies. The whole point of me working my ass off like this is so that she has more choices. Better choices.

She needs to get away from this life. She needs to make it. I don't want her worrying about how to stretch groceries for another week or the art of robbing Peter to pay Paul. I don't want her living like this for the rest of her life. Hell, I don't think I can live this way for another minute.

Every month I have to beg our landlord not to kick us out as I scrounge money together to pay him, and most months I'm usually short. Then my bills take a 'whichever is more important' priority. Electricity is high up there. Then food, gas, water. I usually get all the bills paid without getting them shut off, but not always.

It's the same thing every thirty days. An endless cycle that I can't get ahead of. Once I make some extra money and think that I can finally save and get ahead, that's when my piece of shit car breaks down. So there you have it. Bye-bye extra money.

I'm not good at this. Clearly. I wish more than anything that my parents were still alive. They left Terrica and me a few years ago by way of death from a car accident. That first year without them was the hardest twelve months I'd ever had to deal with, and while I'd like to say things are getting easier, that would be a lie. I think it's more like I'm becoming immune to the way life wants to use me and spit me out.

And then today happens.

I lost my job. It was unexpected but not surprising if that makes any sense. Now I'm really going to have to scramble. Being young, black, and an unemployed woman in the middle of Texas is hard as shit. Finding a job will not be easy. Especially once you throw into the mix my lack of college education and experience.

It's the Catch-22 of the ages. No job, no experience. No experience, no job.

"Let me find a job," Terrica says. "Let me help."

For once it's not the most ridiculous thing I've ever heard of. For once, I want to buckle from the pressure and allow her to help, but then common sense and maybe a little bit of pride kicks in. I can't let her risk graduating high school on time just to help me out. I made a promise to my parents. Graduation for Terrica is the goal.

"It'll be fine. I'm sure something will come up. I've got a couple of irons in the fire."

"Kennedy, you're being crazy. I can work and go to school. Many kids my age do it all the time."

"Many of those kids don't need five hours of study time either."

I shake my head, glaring at her with my best 'let's drop the subject' look.

"It's senior year, Kennedy. I don't even have that many credits left. I won't have to study as hard as I had to last year."

"Oh, we're playing that game? Like it's so easy for you to get good grades. I have a final report card on file from last year that begs to differ. You need all the time you can get to knock these last few credits out and graduate. No distractions. No job."

Terrica rolls her eyes and snatches her history textbook off the dining room table.

"Fine, but I really wish you'd let me help."

I smile to myself because I can tell that she believes that things aren't as bad as they seem. I must be putting on a good act because things are actually that bad. Even though I really should let her get a part-time job after school to help us- I won't. I made a promise. School comes first.

"It'll be ok. If you just do your part, we'll be fine."

Like most teenagers, Terrica is distracted by everything like television, her cell phone, boys, music, and makeup. Sometimes I'm envious of how oblivious she is to the real world. The adult world. A harsh and unforgiving world that I purposely shield her from. Sometimes I wish I could live that cluelessly but I can't.

"I'm going to bed." She walks off to her room and I sigh.

I need to think of something to do and quickly, or she and I will be out on the streets very soon. I consider calling the one auntie who checks in on us now and then, but then I quickly decide against making the call. She has her own family to feed.

I grab the newspaper, glancing over the classifieds, trying my best to find anything that can make me some quick money, fast. An hour later, when I've circled more than half the job opportunities, I turn out the light and head off to bed. Maybe tomorrow will be better. Maybe tomorrow something will fall into my lap.

As I lay my head to sleep, I pray. Yes, I pray to anyone listening that somehow we get out of this mess we're in. Tomorrow will be better. Tomorrow I'll figure out this mess. Tomorrow I'll find a way to figure it all out. I have to.

I smile to myself, knowing that it can't get any worse. It just can't. I hoped that my last job would have lasted a little longer, but that's okay. I still have faith. I know I can do it. Rent is due, along with a mountain of other bills, but I've got this. I'll figure it out.

Maybe I'll step outside of the box. Maybe I'll try something different. Can't hurt, right? The bills pile up no matter what I do, so I might as well get crazy with it.

Funny thing though, before I can do anything of the sort, my sister has beaten me to it. Why doesn't she ever listen?

CHAPTER TWO

VIKTOR

"BOSS, THE NEW RECRUITS ARE HERE," Nicholai, my second in command, says after he cracks the door open to my office.

"Any good prospects?" I ask, saving a document really quick to my computer so I can shut it down before getting started with the interviews.

I've learned from experience to keep anything personal as far away from the new recruits as I can. The high-class strippers I deal with are one tax document away from running me into the ground. I trust no one, especially the women who work for me.

Just because they take their clothes off for more money than your average hole-in-the-wall dive bar, doesn't mean they are any more trustworthy.

"The first one is fucking hot, and I want a shot at her after you're done with her. The second is acting like a fucking queen, so fuck that. And the third one hasn't shown up yet."

"When the late one gets here, send her in. You know how I feel about disrespect."

I hate when people are late, especially when they are late for an appointment with me. My time is precious. My time costs me money. It is one of the few things I agree with the man I call my father about. When she gets here she is going to wish she didn't even bother showing up. Because tardiness is not in my game plan.

The one thing Nicholai doesn't realize is he thinks I am busy screwing these girls into high heaven during each interview, but I'm not. Not even close. It's all perception. And, being an asshole is one of my best features. It gains me respect in my world, and it also makes people afraid to question anything I do.

"You got it, boss," Nicholai smirks with understanding. "I'll send in the first one."

When Nicholai closes my door, I run my hand over my stubbled jaw. I am not in the mood for this shit today. I want to go home, open a nice bottle of red, and chill.

Texas became prime Bratva territory when Boris moved here. For some people, when they think of the mob, they automatically picture some New Jersey schmuck with money stashed away at his mistress's house. That kind of thinking is fine by me. It allows me to conduct my business and stay under the radar, exactly where I like to be.

My business is no longer as cut-throat as Boris, the man who had taken me in and I call my father, made it. When he was murdered, I beat the shit out of anyone that tried to take my rightful place as the head of the business. Many challenged me. Mostly because I wasn't a blood relative. Yet after some broken knuckles and hospital visits, soldiers in the Bratva figured out really fast that they weren't taking this away from me. Some even call me a monster. I don't give a fuck.

As soon as I earned the respect I deserved, I started erasing the shit Boris had gotten us into. My first task was getting rid of all the fucking drugs he had shipped in. The thing about living in Texas? The

Mexican border is close. Real close. Drug trafficking is a walk in the damn park, and the park is all mine. But I am determined not to go out as Boris had. No, I want to be classier. Smarter. I want to build, to grow. I want no part of illegal drugs.

Street drugs are easy money, but they put you on everybody's fucking radar, and, as I said, that is somewhere I don't like to be. So I cleaned up the town, got rid of all our heavy drug affiliation, and here we are. Sitting pretty.

Don't think I'm some softy though. My new business turned us away from the prying eye of the district attorney, but having Mexico so close is still a gold mine, and I am a fucking miner. So instead of hard drugs, I smuggle other drugs. Yeah, yeah, I know...I'm a hypocrite. I already told you that I'm an asshole.

Now we deal with antibiotics and pain pills. The real drugs in America. Everyone knows that if they need something they can come to my pharmacist, Gary. Gary is the fifth pharmacist I have been through since taking over the business. The other ones, well, let's just say they needed to prescribe some pretty heavy stuff to breathe comfortably. So far, Gary has been the most trustworthy. He only prescribes drugs to the people who need it. No more glassy-eyed, pill-popping druggies looking for a fix. Just businessmen in suits and PTO moms. This is my business, and business is good.

Nicholai sticks his head in and gives me a wink before opening my door wide. A curvy little piece with huge tits saunters in on six-inch hot pink stiletto heels. She is wearing a matching hot pink dress with cutouts on the sides, her breasts straining to get out, and those hips jut out the holes just begging to be gripped as she is being pounded from behind.

"What's your name?" I ask, my cock doing some straining of its own. Hey, come on don't hate--she's practically naked here.

"Kandi," she answers, batting her too thick with mascara clumpy fucking eyelashes. She didn't even try to put on some more natural-looking fake eyelashes like my other girls. No, she just painted on some cheap makeup. As if that is going to impress me.

Tits and body? Impressive.

Skin and the vanilla fragrance of her skin, also impressive.

Not putting in the extra effort to please me ... no fucking way.

She is so low-trash, low rent. Not at all like the upscale girls, I generally hire to 'perform'.

"Nope, we already have a Kandi. Sorry, you'll have to try again."

I lean back and let my eyes roam over her smoking hot body, all curves, and hills. Sure, I already know that I'm not going to hire her, but I want to have a little fun. And, not the her sucking my dick kind. Although, that's what Nicholai always thinks that I do back here in my office. He reveres me as a God, wanting so badly to be me. Ha, who wouldn't?

Kandi pouts and then brushes her pink-tipped fingernail over her bottom lip. I guess she thinks by sucking me off she might get the job, 'cause that's the vibe I am getting from her.

Just the thought makes me feel better. My mood has been off for a week now. In fact, the reason I am interviewing new talent has to do with my pissed off attitude. One of my girls recently overdosed on heroin, which means someone is dealing fucking street drugs into my territory. When I find out who is undermining my authority, they are going to be a dead motherfucker. I don't tolerate disrespect.

"Don't pout, sweetheart," I snicker. "We can find you another name. Besides, I'm sure you can think of something better to do with those lips in my office," I tease her.

She smiles as her greedy eyes land on the zipper holding back my dick. She licks her glossy cotton candy-colored lips and moves closer to me. My feet swivel me around so she can get a better angle.

I can't believe I am carrying this on so far. I need to just boot her out of my office and stop wasting time. What the fucks wrong with me?

"Anything you want, Sir," she whispers, getting down on her knees.

I hook a finger under her chin, drawing her in a little closer as I whisper back, "Anything, hmm?"

She takes an unsteady breath. "Yes, Sir."

"Say that again."

"Yes, Sir."

I pause for a moment, looking at her face, then roam my eyes over her sexy as fuck cleavage.

"Wear this dress for me, did you?"

"Yes, Sir."

I caress my thumb across the swell of her tits, then down slowly across her nipple until she moans softly under my touch.

"You want me to fuck you so badly, don't you?"

"Y-Yes, Sir."

She is panting and I am about to fucking break

my own rules for the sake of relieving my needful cock that can't stop throbbing as I touch and look at her. She is fucking low rent but still beautiful ... horrible makeup and all.

I need to fucking stop this.

Now.

"Then," I begin, moving my fingers back under her chin, "you should have come into my office with a bit more respect for me ... and maybe even yourself."

She gulps. "Sir?"

"Time to go now, Kandi. Get up."

She rises to her feet in a hurry, huffing and throwing a little tantrum the whole while.

"I can't believe you!" she exclaims.

"Believe it. Now get out." I am bored already with her and my whole game of teasing her. "I have another girl coming in right now. Sorry, but I don't think you're Bliss material."

"What the fuck?" she screams as she glances around the room, taking in my collection of Cuban cigar cases.

"Thank you for stopping by," I tell her, rising from my seat.

"This is bullshit," she spits, her hand flying for my face.

Shaking my head, I grab her wrist and hold it

tightly. "I suggest you rethink what you're about to do. It won't end well. Now turn the fuck around and get the hell out of my office."

She jerks her wrist free and stomps toward the door, slamming it on her way out.

CHAPTER THREE

VIKTOR

SHIT, I didn't want to be here dealing with this. Unfortunately, I have no choice. Having someone dealing drugs in my territory means this needs to be handled directly by me. No one is going to slip by again.

Nicholai returns with a smile on his face. "I guess it didn't go well. Damn, I really wanted to play with those big tits."

"Too much trailer trash in her. She wasn't cut out."

"You're an asshole, Viktor," he says with a look of adoration.

"Yeah," I say, adjusting my silver tie. "Tell me something I don't already know."

I know I am the biggest fucking dick on the planet. Yet, people respect me anyway, and if they don't, I take care of it until they do.

"I have something that will make you feel better. The late one just showed up."

"Send her in," I tell him against my better judgment

Minutes later, a petite girl with a jean mini skirt and a black tube top walks in. Her skin is just as warm looking as the "Kandi" before her. Long honey-colored hair too. Not sure if it's real or not, but it doesn't matter, she's definitely attractive. I rub my eyes and try to blink, to clear my fucking thoughts of lust.

Then I stupidly let my eyes linger on her curvy legs, thinking of the different positions I could get them in. Or, at least that's what I am thinking until I look at her face. Her scared, underage face with frightened whiskey-colored eyes. This girl isn't like Kandi. This needed to end immediately. I don't hire kids.

"Get the fuck out," I tell her matter of factly.

What the hell is Nicholai thinking by letting a damn minor into my club?

"Wait," she trembles moving closer to me. "Please let me show you what I can do," she says, tears welling in her eyes. "I need the work."

Before I can kick the kid out, my door flies open with a fury fueled woman and a flustered Nicholai following behind her.

Ah, fuck.

The doorknob smacks the wall and rebounds, almost knocking into the petite girl.

"Get away from my sister!" she roars.

Her slim finger points straight at me while her eyes skim over her sister to see just how much innocence she has shed before arriving to rescue her.

"Sorry, boss." Nicholai huffs, "She snuck around me and I couldn't catch her," he apologizes.

I glare at the woman who has barged into my office.

Fuck.

A mix of dark brown and honey-colored curls with skin just as warm and inviting, like a fucking dessert bar on legs. Honey, Caramel and chocolate. The hair is real, and so is the sexiness, and this one isn't frightened at all.

Goddamn.

I want a taste.

"Kennedy, what the hell are you doing here?" the

kid, who I assume is the sister based on their similar features, asks.

"You don't get to ask questions," her sister shoots back. "I didn't drop out of college and work two jobs just so your stupid ass could become a stripper." She shoots me a look. "Definitely not for a man like him."

Her breath hitches just a bit when her attention lands on me. It isn't the first time a woman reacted like this to me. I am a sexy motherfucker, but this is the first time I have had a similar reaction.

Sure, lots of women give me hard-ons and make me want to bury myself balls deep into their wet pussies, but this is different.

She has the same large whiskey-colored eyes as her sister but hers are more pronounced because of the dark bags underneath them. Her hair is thrown haphazardly on her head. She is skin and bones and looks like she is about to pass out from exhaustion if it weren't for the anger pushing her. Having said all of that though...she is still fucking beautiful.

She needs to get away from me. Far away from me. I don't have time for distractions, and this chick and her sister are tons of distractions.

"Take your sister and get the hell out of my office," I tell her with a bored tone in my voice. If only my dick was actually this bored.

"We're going," Kennedy, the tiny terror, says.

"No, I'm interviewing for a position, Kennedy."

"The hell you are, Terrica," Kennedy says, trying to pull her sister out of my office as Nicholai and I watch quietly. I can't believe this shit is happening. I don't really do family drama. Yet it's unfolding all right before my eyes.

"Yes, I want this job. You are going to kill yourself working so much. A person needs more than one to two hours of sleep a night. Without mom and dad, you are all I have. I can't lose you too."

The tears that have been threatening to fall since the younger girl walked into my office finally got their wish and fell freely down her heavily made-up face.

Ah, fuck. This circus in my office needs to be over, but I couldn't stop watching. It was like a bad reality TV show or a car accident. I couldn't look away. Neither could Nicholai.

"Terrica, I'm fine." She pulls the young girl in and hugs her tightly. "I told you, I got this."

What the fuck is happening in my office? A therapy session?

"Let's get out of this man's office. I'm sure he doesn't want to listen to our family drama."

Kennedy turns her tired worn-out face toward

me and winks. My cock immediately jumps against my zipper. Tired as shit, and she is still hot as fuck.

"It's not the worst that has been in here." I wink back and then a blush creeps across her cheeks.

Oh fuck. Innocence. It has been a long time since I've seen innocence. Mine had been lost at the age of twelve, the first time I saw a man scream in pain before a bullet sliced his head open.

I want hers.

Without another word, she grabs her sister and pulls her out of my office.

"Should I send in the next one?" Nicholai asks. Oblivious to how I've just been shaken to the core by this woman.

"Why the hell would you send in a kid?" I ask, leaning over my desk, my anger ready to burst out.

"A kid?"

Idiot.

"*Tupitsa* (dumbass), that girl couldn't have been older than sixteen. Luckily I was ready to kick her ass out before her sister came storming in, but you let her in."

I think again about the gorgeous woman who swooped through here like a hurricane. The sister looked like she was dead on her feet. The sister that had my cock wanting to jump off my body so it could go live happily inside her.

"Shit, I didn't even notice," Nicholai says, rubbing his buzzed black hair.

"Tell the next one that she has the job and not to fuck it up," I tell him.

"Got it."

Before Nicholai closes my door, I stop him. My back teeth clench together before the words I would probably regret are forced out.

"Find out everything about her."

"About who?"

"The hurricane."

CHAPTER FOUR

VIKTOR

"THIS IS WHERE SHE LIVES? Of course. It fucking figures." I stare at the documents in front of me.

"What are you thinking?" Nicholai asks.

I seek his eyes for a moment and then return back to the documents at hand. Thing is, I don't want to tell him my thoughts, because I didn't even understand them.

All I know is, her innocence mixed with her determination sparked something in me. The business I deal in doesn't allow me to feel anything. Feelings are for pussies. The minute emotions come into play, you are dead. After a while, you forget what it feels like to be human. Like a constant flatline. I want a daily dose from her pure sweetness to get me high.

It is a high only she can offer.

After Kennedy, otherwise known as Kennedy Howard, and her sister Terrica left my office, I made it Nicholai's priority to find out everything he could. Three hours after she left, I had her life story in front of me, printed neatly in black and white. Kennedy is twenty-three. Two years ago she took full custody of her, then, fourteen-year-old sister, Terrica.

Fucking Nicholai had let in a sixteen-year-old in my office. Tupitsa. (Dumbass) I swear he's going to get the club shut down one day.

Their story is fucked up. Their parents had been killed by a drunk driver on New Year's Eve. So Kennedy had to drop out of her last semester of college and take on three jobs to help pay for the funeral expenses and care of her sister.

Anger surges through me as I scan over the woman's work schedule. Terrica hadn't been kidding when she said her sister had only been sleeping two hours a night.

"I'm going to her house." I push my chair back, rising to my feet.

"It's after midnight," Nicholai hedged. "Your big Russian ass is going to her neighborhood at this time of night? I think you're going to stick out like a sore thumb."

"I don't care." My sapphire-blue eyes grow darker as I stare him down.

"I'll bring the car around."

He leaves my office as I straighten my tie. Nicholai is smart enough to keep his mouth shut, even though I know his opinion of what I am about to do.

I have a plan.

Money talks and I have plenty of it. Two facts that Kennedy Howard is about to become acquainted with.

CHAPTER FIVE

KENNEDY

A STRIPPER? I can't believe Terrica is stupid enough to think that stripping is the solution. I may not know exactly what the answer is, but one thing I do know is that dancing for slimeballs and money isn't it.

I wish I could tell her what the solution for us actually is because all I am setting an example for is work, work, and some more work. If I'm lucky, I might die before the doctor bills catch up, because working three (oh wait, it's only two now) jobs will be the death of me. How much more can I handle? Not much more.

After our parents died, I was overwhelmed with all the responsibilities it took to raise my sister and keep a roof over our heads. Our parents were relatively young and not huge planners, so there was no insurance money, no will, nothing.

Unfortunately, we weren't born into wealth, and when they died my reality quickly changed. College would have to be put on hold. Working full-time was the only solution. Unfortunately, I didn't have the credentials to secure a good-paying full-time gig in an office or somewhere like that, so I picked as many part-time jobs as I could. I never have a day off. I never am able to enjoy the 'simple' things in life. No, I am the rat in the rat race people talk about.

And with all the hours I work, I definitely could never find a man. Relationships are just not in the cards for me. I don't even try to look. Honestly, I am in debt up to my eyeballs, so I can't even think about a man. I like to look though.

The owner at the strip club, whew, he was so good-looking. That accent? Panty melting. But I already know that he isn't a good man so it kind of cancels all of that sexiness out. I mean what kind of man owns a strip club? What kind of man would allow an underage girl to work for him? A monster and a predator, that's who.

"Terrica, promise me you'll never do anything that stupid again."

We walk down the shabby hallway to our apartment. Depressing. The wallpaper is cracking and peeling, and in many places, it's torn off completely. The threadbare tan carpet under our feet appears as if it has been walked on for ages, and one of the overhead lights has burned out. Home sweet home.

Terrica looks over at me, regret filling her eyes. "I'm sorry. I just thought I could help."

"Help me by going to school and getting good grades," I say, placing the key into the rusty lock of our front door. "Help me by graduating."

"Okay." She nudges me. "But, did you get a look at the man who owns the club? Mr. Petrov? He was criminally hot." She waves her hand in front of her face as she smiles.

Shaking my head, I push the door open. "Criminally hot?"

I throw my keys on the entryway table as Terrica follows me inside our tiny apartment.

"Yeah, like he'd be arrested if anyone saw how hot he was."

"Um, that makes no sense."

"You got something against Russian guys?"

"I don't have time for any guy and neither do you. Go to bed."

I slide my purse from my shoulder as I step into the kitchen.

"I'm not tired. I'm going to watch TV, night." She kisses my cheek as she rushes back to her bedroom.

In our one-bedroom apartment, Terrica has the only room with a small TV.

I, on the other hand, have a bed in the corner of the living room with a shower curtain separating me from the couch.

Removing my heels and changing into my nightclothes, I sink into my small mattress and decide to get a few hours sleep before my shift at the gas station down the street.

As I snuggle under the blanket, my thoughts drift to the man I met face to face tonight. The criminally hot Viktor Petrov. Everyone knows who he is. It is no mystery who he is or the fact that he owns Club Bliss. Texas might be big but our town is relatively small.

Mr. Petrov's father was a criminal, so it's safe to assume that he is probably a criminal, too. I don't know much about the mob, but I do know that his father ran it. And I know to stay away from anyone associated with him. Especially the son.

He is gorgeous but scary. Pretty, but ugly. Oh, so good, but so so bad. His magnetic color-changing eyes never wavered from mine as he sat perched in his chair, yelling at us to leave. He intimidated me, to the point I wanted to run away and cry which, we pretty much did.

His muscles are huge. Bigger than most men in town. Although he had a suit on, I am totally aware of the tattoos covering every inch of his skin underneath it. Sure, I've read a few magazine articles on the guy. That's how I know. Never thought I'd meet him though.

But I did.

And, he is prettier in person.

I close my eyes, imagining his strong hands on my body. His beard tickling the inside of my thighs. My hand moves to the spot between my thighs, over my panties, wishing it was his strong hand instead. The way he stared at me plays through my mind over and over. It was hot. He was hot.

And his voice turned me on something fierce. That deep, gravely, Russian accent peppered with a Texas twang is something special.

I begin to rub my fingers over the panel of my soaked panties. This man could probably give me things I haven't had in years. It's been so long since

I've felt a man touch me. Since I've had a man inside me.

I slip my panties to the side, letting my thin fingers enter me, making me wetter than I already am. I imagine Viktor's fingers inside me instead. I want this man to touch me. What is wrong with me? He was going to hire my little sister to dance for him. Isn't he the anti-Christ?

I try not to let my mind wander to how wrong this is. Instead, I focus on the way his lips curved when he first saw me. The way his eyes roamed over my entire body like he couldn't get his fill. He was attracted to me. Even looking my worst- he wanted me.

My fingers pick up speed, wanting more than anything to have these thoughts of Viktor to make me come. It was insane.

I moan into the room, trying my best to keep it down. I play with my clit, bucking my hips against my hand.

My mind drifts back to the exchange we shared tonight. The way he stared at me causes chills to race over my skin. It was hot.

I imagine Viktor's tongue inside me, bringing me closer and closer to an orgasm. I imagine him grabbing my ass in his large hands, his mouth devouring me, his cock getting harder by tasting me.

I want him to have it. To have me. I want him to take everything he wants in the dominant way I know he would. The release of control is one thing I wish for, but could never act on. How could I? Especially with him.

He isn't the type of man I should even be thinking about it. But here I am, thinking about having his mouth on me, his tongue deep inside me as far as it could go, making me see stars.

I plunge another finger inside me, trying my best to hit those certain spots inside me, making me wetter and wetter. God, I wonder what he would feel like. I wonder how good he'd be.

"Viktor," I whisper into the night, hoping more than anything I'd see him again. But, I can't. That would be insane.

I imagine myself dancing for him in his club. His eyes following me as they did in his office. His eyes gazing right through me, wanting me, willing me to do wicked things. More than anything I want those eyes on me again. Fuck, how could someone so bad make me want him like this?

My fingers keep moving. My thoughts growing

dirtier. I want it. I imagine I have it. I imagine him with his rock hard dick running it along my wetness.

"Fuck," I moan.

My body is so close to coming all over my hand. I am just so close to imagining Viktor giving me everything I haven't had in so long. I'm ninety-nine percent sure he'd do a good job of it too.

At the first sight of my orgasm, I roll over, biting onto my pillow, silencing the moan I want to let out. My body crumbles, my orgasm rolling through every cell in my body. I imagine Viktor's smile when he sees me getting off to his fingers inside me. To me dancing for him. To him fucking me harder than he has ever fucked in his life.

I want all of it. I want all of him. But, I know it will never ever happen. It should never happen. I met the man once. What the hell am I thinking? This is just my poor, dusty, vagina talking.

My body starts to relax, my breathing coming back down as the orgasm subsides. I remove my hand, wishing more than anything Viktor could be here to lick my release off my fingers.

Gah, I read too many dirty books.

I am pathetic. I am lusting after a man I will never see again. A man I can never have. A man I shouldn't even want.

I make my way to the bathroom, and clean myself up, heading back to my room to try to get some sleep before my early shift tomorrow. As soon as my head hits the pillow, a loud banging sounds at the front door.

"Terrica, are you okay?" I call out, bounding from the bed.

Another loud knock and I race to the door, wondering who in the world could be here this late at night. If it is one of Terrica's friends I will not be happy.

With no peephole, I cautiously open the door and am met with the same piercing eyes I'd been thinking about just moments before. The same eyes I swore I would never see again. What is he doing here? And the way his eyes are smiling at me, I swear that he knows what I was doing only minutes before.

Remembering the criminal that I'm dealing with, I harden, putting up a wall around myself.

"What the hell are you doing here?"

CHAPTER SIX

VIKTOR

THE DOOR to her shitty apartment has a dingy-flowered welcome mat in front of it. I'm not sure if it has seen better days or if it has been thrown out in the world looking like that. I give a rap on the door. I don't even know this woman, but I hate that she lives here. I hate being here as well.

A few minutes later, Kennedy blinks wearily as she stares at me through the chain lock. She is blushed, out of breath, and oh my fuck, didn't my dick twitch at the sight of her. She is sexy fresh out of bed, and my mind races, thinking about what I can do to her there.

"What are you doing here?" she asks through the crack.

"It's nice to see you too. May I come in?" I eye the flimsy chain knowing I or anyone else could break it with one solid push to the door, and I almost want to just to get closer to her.

She must realize the same thing because she shuts the door slightly and releases the chain. When she opens the door wide, I am greeted with two very visible nipples through a threadbare white shirt. Fuck. How am I not supposed to look? So, I don't try to. I shamelessly stare at her and smile when I noticed she is wearing Spongebob panties.

She clears her throat, trying to cover herself with her hands. "Eyes up here."

Those panties need to be on the floor at my feet while I fuck her senseless.

"But they like being down there. Other things besides my eyes wouldn't mind being down there," I tell her with a smirk, watching the blush creep up her cheeks. God, she is turning me on.

There it is again, innocence painting her cheeks scarlet. Not virginal innocence like the sister, but rather a lack of experience. It's clear that she hasn't been with a real man. Only boys.

"Can you please explain why you are at my

house at twelve-thirty in the morning, eye-fucking me, and saying inappropriate things, or do you just want me to call the cops?"

She may have been serious, but I still couldn't help the smile spreading across my face. Then the irony of the situation strikes me and the smile immediately vacates my face.

"Why the fuck did you answer the door? Fuck, you are practically naked," I growl at her.

This time my eyes sweep over her entire body, but instead of getting turned on, it angers me. What is she thinking? Most men who could come to her door wouldn't be as well-mannered as me. Anyone could do who knows what to her, and here she is stupidly answering the door like there aren't bad men out there. I know I'm a bad man, I never said I wasn't, but I would never force myself on anyone. I've never had to. I've never wanted to. It's usually the reverse. Most women beg to let me make them come.

I push the errant thoughts from my mind, as she parks a hand on her thin hip.

"What the hell. You were banging on my door in the middle of the night." She crosses her arms, making her tits more pronounced. "I didn't exactly have time to get dressed."

"What if it was a rapist or a killer? You're just going to let them in?"

Fuck, my anger and her tits in that shirt were making my dick hard.

"Are you a rapist or killer?" she asks sarcastically.

I lean against the wall, crossing my arms. "Not a rapist."

She gasps, and for the first time, fear sparks in her hardened eyes.

"Don't worry, I'm not going to murder you. Promise. I'm here to make you an offer. One you'll like." I hoped.

Her fingers start to toy with the ends of her t-shirt, pulling it down, trying to cover herself. What the fuck is wrong with me? Why did that simple act turn me on? I can't turn away from the action. My dick is growing in my pants, and I need to tamper down this action. I move to the other side of the room, leaning on the far wall this time.

"What kind of offer?" she asks, innocently, ever so cute.

Pushing off the wall, I cross the small living room. I can't stand still in here. The small space is suffocating me. Squalor. Although she has made an effort to minimize the worn blue sofa with a colorful throw draped on the back, and fresh flowers on the beat-up wooden coffee table. Family pictures adorn the wall, and I cross over to the tiny counter in the galley-style kitchen.

I admire her for the effort. At least she was trying to make this place look like a home on whatever she earned. At least she was standing on her own two feet trying to care for her little sister. I can see there is more to her than just bad circumstances. I can tell there is something special within her, and that thought has me here in the middle of the night. It has me obsessing over her.

"What's going on? What's he doing here?" Terrica asks, coming out of the single door I noticed in the apartment. Her face is void of make-up and she is wearing a My Little Pony t-shirt and looks very much like an innocent sixteen-year-old. Much different than in the club.

"Grab the stuff that is most valuable." I look around the tiny apartment figuring the task wouldn't take more than ten minutes' tops. "Both of you."

"What the hell are you talking about, Mr. uhh?" Kennedy arches her eyebrow asking for my name as if she doesn't know it already.

"Petrov...the name is Viktor Petrov and as I said, I have an offer for you."

"Well, I don't have sex with strange men for money, if that's what you're thinking."

I probably could have been suaver at handing out the offer, but I am still fucking pissed she answered the door and let me in so easily.

"That's not the offer, although if you'd like to negotiate that into the deal, I'm down." I laugh.

"Highly unlikely," she says with narrowed eyes.

"Really? Because it seems like you've been thinking about it."

"Puh-lease."

"Get your things," I chuckle. "It's late and I'd like to get home." I lean against the counter waiting for the two of them to pack.

"Can we hear this offer? Or is it a mystery?"

"I'm hiring you. And, no employee of mine lives in the hood. Therefore, you'll be staying with me until I find somewhere suitable for you to live."

"This is not the hood, thank you very fucking much, and I resent you for calling it that."

"Yeah, me too!" the teenager chimes in.

"I mean no disrespect, but I know what this neighborhood once was and what it is today. I know there are probably some very nice families still on this block, but I also know every place where they sell drugs within a five-mile radius. You can't stay here."

"But..." she protests.

"It's best to be doing what I say...*Potoropis*."

"What does that mean?" Terrica asks.

"It means hurry the fuck up."

Kennedy glares at me, immobile and probably too fucking stunned to speak. I want to snap my fingers at her, to move her along, but I rake my eyes over her body instead. My offer was probably delivered a little rough around the edges, but I can tell she is seriously considering it. She wants a way out. I can tell. She just has to step up and take it.

"Get the shit that means anything to you. Don't worry about anything else. I'll replace it," I tell her digging myself even deeper. "Please," I add. Hoping that will help.

She finally hops to it, and her and Terrica both walk away to pack.

My instincts tell me that this simple decision is going to change my life. At this point though, I'm not sure if it will be in a good or bad way. I've never done anything like this before. Right now, I'm going by the seat of my pants, and I hope that I will get her in the seat of my pants soon enough.

I figure after I get my fill of her (because I always

do), I could set her up in a better apartment, help her with her finances, and get her the hell out of my mind. It'll be a win-win for both of us.

"I need to know what 'll be doing for you? I don't strip, and I'm not going to sleep with you." The look on her face almost makes me laugh, but she is serious. So cute.

"Don't worry, I had Nicholai look into you. I know everything. I also know you were about to graduate with your business degree. I need someone I can trust to help me with some business situations, and I'm hiring you. I'll pay you, and you two can stay at my house rent-free."

"You asshole. You can't just bust in here in the middle of the night, tell me and my sister to pack our shit and then dictate how I will be living my life." The volume of her voice shows me that she no longer cares if Terrica or the rest of the apartment complex hears her.

"I'm an asshole? No sweetheart, I'm saving you from a dire situation. I know you're about two seconds away from getting evicted."

She contemplates my truthful words for a moment as she angrily continues to pack. Here I thought she would have gotten down on her knees and sucked my dick for saving her. Instead, she is arguing with me as if I did something wrong offering her a sweet ass deal to get out of the shit debt her parents have left her in.

"Kennedy, let's just go with him. The gas got turned off three days ago. I haven't had a hot shower in forever."

"I told you that I was taking care of it."

"How? When you won't let me help. Look, Mr. Petrov is offering you a job, a real job, and he knows what he is getting into. Please."

Kennedy looks over at her sister who has two full duffle bags on the floor next to her. Her eager eyes must have been the clincher. Kennedy's slim shoulders sink down and her weary face takes on a look of defeat.

"Give me twenty more minutes, and go sit on the couch. I have to talk to Mr. Petrov," she tells her sister.

Terrica smiles and skips to the couch, her duffle bags banging into her legs as she moves.

"Viktor, call me Viktor," I say as I follow her into the room her sister just exited.

"What do you want from me?" she whispers once she closes the door and starts tossing her things into a worn-out backpack. "Seriously, now. What do you want?"

"I want you to help me get my business in order. From what I have read, you are an excellent employee. Naive, but excellent."

"What do you mean naive?" she asks, her head whipping toward me.

"Naive because you work extra hard, but in the two years you have been working for three companies, you have never once asked for a raise. You think working harder is going to get you what you want in this world. That's what's naive about you."

"I'm not sure what they teach in Russia, but in America, hard work is considered a valuable trait. A badge of honor."

"I've lived in America long enough to know what's valued here, and don't get me wrong, I respect what you've done. You're a hard worker, and I need people like you around me. I need people I can trust," I tell her, leaning against the wall, waiting for her to finally thank me for my generosity.

She opens her mouth and snaps it closed as my words finally hit her.

"I'm not naive, and I'm not going to sleep with you." Her dark eyes narrow on me. "That's clearly what this is about."

I couldn't help but give her a toothy smile. She is

going to sleep with me. It's inevitable. I can smell the pheromones bouncing around this room all over the place.

"I never said anything about sex. It seems you're the one thinking about it."

She grits her teeth, and her eyes shoot to my crotch before coming back to my face. "I'm not thinking about it. Besides, what makes you think you can trust me?" she throws back, turning around to continue packing.

"Instinct," I tell her, shouldering the backpack and the other bag she has packed. "Are you ready?" I ask, heading for the door.

"Yes," she answers my back.

"Good, because I'm tired. Come on, Terrica, let's get you out of this hell hole."

"Shut up, that's my house you're talking about," Kennedy says as I throw their shit in the back of my car.

"Oh please, get in," I tell her almost unable to hide the smile that wants to appear. "I'm about to take you to a *real* house."

CHAPTER SEVEN

VIKTOR

I SIP my whiskey laced coffee in the dining room thinking about what I've just done. I brought a woman and a teenager into my home with no real plan. All because my dick won't take no for an answer. Boris would kill me.

Kennedy fell asleep as soon as I started the car last night. Terrica has been useful by telling me that she hadn't been sleeping well at night with all the stress of having multiple jobs. With all the stress this life has unfairly thrown her way. I could only imagine. I've never understood this kind of life, Boris gave me a great one, but I can tell it hasn't been easy on her.

I carried Kennedy up to the room I had prepared for her and made sure Terrica was settled into the room across the hall. She wasn't too happy when I told her a driver would be taking her to school the next morning, but when I gave her my "boss" look she stopped arguing immediately. I'm definitely not used to having to reign in a teenager, but she can't be any worse than one of my employees. One of my soldiers.

Tell them what to do and don't take no for an answer.

Kennedy slept the entire morning and I checked on her a few times, watching her sleep. I couldn't stop watching her. I like the way her chest would rise and fall in even tempos. I like the way the sun casts its rays across her caramel skin. I especially like the way she would mumble little nothings while she dreamed. I was hoping she'd utter my name. She didn't.

Terrica is scheduled to be back from school in thirty minutes. I check on Kennedy once more, but she hasn't moved from the spot I placed her in last night.

She wrestles slightly, moaning a bit as her eyes

open, taking in her surroundings. "Where?" She sits up, rubbing her eyes. "Where am I?"

"My home," I say, like there would be any other place I would have taken her.

"Why didn't you wake me up?" she asks, taking in the room with the big bed I placed her in last night. "Why would you let me sleep all day?"

"Because you were dead on your feet, and you won't do me any good if you can't stay awake."

"Where is Terrica?" she asks, noticing we are alone.

"She's at school. I had my driver take her, and he is picking her up when she gets out."

"He?"

"Yes, he. And he knows not to lay a hand on her. She's under my protection. No one will touch her."

She should know that. She should know I wouldn't allow anyone to harm her or her sister.

"Must be nice to be a mob boss," she says, then claps her hand over her mouth. "Shit, sorry."

"It's okay. I am a mob boss. So, you're right. And people do as I say." I walk closer to her side of the bed. "Most of the time It is nice."

"Oh," is all she can respond with.

I chuckle at her indignation. Normally, only Nicholai gives me shit and that's because he is like a brother to me. Everyone else is scared of me, and that is the way I like it. That's the way it ought to be. Except, I am enjoying Kennedy's smart mouth. The smart mouth that I want to have wrapped around my fat cock.

My dick twitches at the mere thought.

"Well, now you know what you're getting into." I don't want to hide anything from her. "I'm hoping this is not a deal-breaker."

"As if you've given me any choice at this point. You've brainwashed my sister already, and she's only known you for two seconds."

"That's an exaggeration. The poor girl just wanted a hot shower."

"Do you kill people?" she asks in a tiny voice, making my dick spring to life from the sound of it. Her hooded eyes watch me closely as she waits for my answer.

"No, I don't kill people." *Anymore.*

Her questions are turning me on, her morality getting the best of her. She visibly relaxes when I tell her the truth.

"Well, I know who you are Viktor Petrov. I know you own that strip club, but I know you also deal drugs. You don't have the kind of money you do without doing something along those lines. So I'm just letting you know now, I won't be doing anything illegal."

Her nostrils flare, and I can't believe how turned on I am by her fire. My balls are full, ready to mark her as I come all over her. I can picture it exactly. It will be glorious.

"My father dealt drugs," I correct her. "I cleaned all of that up when I took over." And I don't tolerate street drugs at my clubs. At least not the kind she's talking about.

The look on her face shows me that she doesn't believe me. "Don't get me wrong. I'm not a good guy. I didn't get where I am by being a sweetheart, but you will be safe."

"So, nothing illegal?"

"Are we asking stupid questions now?" I chuckle.

Her eyebrow raises and I wait for her to respond.

"There are no stupid questions. I'm asking if I work for you, am I going to be doing something that will get me thrown in jail? Because I don't look good in orange."

"Much better question. No, my tax returns for Bliss are in excellent order. I keep my club on the up and up. My other business you won't have anything to do with, and just to be clear, you *are* working for me. There is no if."

As if she had a choice.

"What if I don't want to work for you?" she huffs out, her eyes darkening with defiance. "We were getting by just fine without your assistance."

"Where are you going to go? I read up on that landlord. Knowing him your apartment has probably already been rented and you haven't even been out of it for twenty-four hours. Plus you were so far behind in your rent that your credit is shot. You won't find another place that will lease to you. I'm offering you a nice place to stay and an excellent salary. My driver will help you get your sister to and from school, and you will be able to get more than a couple hours of sleep with only one job."

Where is the gratitude? I'm waiting. I hate that she is practically forcing me to bring all this up to her. I hate that this was the truth of the matter. But, she needs to understand that what she was doing wasn't working. That this is a better way. The only way.

I always get what I want.

"Why are you doing this?" The desperation in her voice twists my dark heart a little tighter, and I don't like the hard thump it gives at her plea.

"Stupid question, next." I cross my arms over my broad chest.

"So you're sure that Terrica's at school?" she asks with a confused look after I shut her down.

Her confusion and doubt prickles at my skin. I run this whole state; does she not think I can get a sixteen-year-old to school? Or is she not understanding why I brought her in and handed her a better life on a silver platter? Why couldn't she just take my gift and not question it? Because I didn't even know how to answer her ridiculous question without wanting to punch something.

"Of course I'm sure, although, I'm sure she is going to have some words for you when she gets home."

"Why? What did she do?"

This time it is my turn to be surprised. I assumed she was going to think I have done something wrong. This damn chick is fucking with my head, and the worst thing is, I like it. I like being surprised by what she is going to do or say next.

"I made her change three times before I let my driver take her. She was almost late."

Kennedy throws back her head and laughs. Her long neck is exposed and my dick jumps in my slacks trying to get to her. Thoughts of shoving my cock down her slender throat pulses in my head, and I have to swallow the groan wanting to escape.

"Hearing that is almost worth the amount of complaining I'm going to hear when she gets home. That girl has been a pain in my ass since our parents died. Don't get me wrong, I love her. But, she just won't listen to me. I don't know how you got her to change three times. I couldn't even get her to do it once."

Anger has my dick taking a backseat. I am going to have a talk with that little girl. She is putting her sister through hell and that is unacceptable. In my mind, I've decided I am the only one who will be giving Kennedy hell from now on. Or at least until I get sick of her and set her up in her own place.

The laughing inside my head at my plans for Kennedy is ignored. I am a fucking mob boss. Some tiny little thing isn't going to change my views. This is not a forever plan. This is just temporary. Until I'm sick of her.

Kennedy sits down across from me, tucking her legs under her as she props her hands on her chin trying to wake up from probably the most sleep she's had in years.

"You know this is strange, right?" she asks, bringing me back from a fantasy of fucking her on the table while I watch her tits bounce before my lips cover her nipples.

"Do I look like I care?"

Her lips rise as my staff brings in an array of deli sandwiches. Kennedy's stomach growls loud enough that the noise bounces off the walls. I want to feed her before feeding her something else.

"You eat. You're too skinny. I'll fatten you up," Dottie, the lady that runs my house, clucks over her like a mother hen.

Her silver hair is pulled back in a severe bun and her blurry eyes stare at Kennedy until she takes a bite of the sandwich in front of her. When Kennedy moans her approval, Dottie nods her head with satisfaction before walking out of the room.

"So, what do you want me to do?" Kennedy asks after she polishes off her food before I've even finished half of mine.

"Well, I would like you to strip off your clothes, suck my dick, getting it nice and wet before you climb on the table and let me fuck you while you scream my name."

My eyes lock on hers as I watch the heat surface on her cheeks. Interesting that no anger rose, but rather a flicker of interest washes over her before she chokes on the swallow of iced tea she has just taken. It takes her a moment to get herself back together, but the blush on her face doesn't leave.

Very interesting.

"I meant work," she says sternly.

It doesn't matter that she avoided what I said. Her pussy is going to be mine, and it is going to be mine soon. Her eyes don't lie.

"Come on. I'll show you." I stand and purposely adjust myself giving her a show of what she will be getting soon. Her eyes pop at my large bulge and I smirk, sending her a wink when she glances at my face.

She moves to pick up her plate, and I stop her. "Dottie will get it. She runs this place, and you don't want to disrespect her by doing her work for her."

Kennedy nods quietly as I lead her to the office she will be working in. The office that will be right across from mine. I've never seen her this quiet before.

Obviously, I've given her something to think about.

CHAPTER EIGHT

VIKTOR

IT'S BEEN ALMOST two weeks now and having Kennedy in this house is stifling. Like a goddamn elephant sitting on me. I feel her presence bearing down on what's left of my conscience everywhere.

It gives me a headache---she gives me a headache.

I jam my thumbs into my temples, trying to drive her condemning brown eyes out of my head. Fuck. She is still there.

Krissy peeks her head into my open office door. "Everything's all set up for your trip."

"Has Davoff secured everything?" I ask. It's a

needless question. He is a damn genius in technology, with a knack for hacking into anything undetected. She nods yes.

"Good, when he gets here, I want to see him first thing."

"Of course." She steps inside. Krissy has been my personal assistant for five years. She doesn't question things, she doesn't complain, if I need something tomorrow, it's done today, and I know from the slight twist of her lips something is up. "So, I know you wanted to give Kennedy some work to do..."

I wait for her to finish. She does that a lot. Leaving me in suspense. It's a small price to pay for an employee who doesn't question that I now have a woman and her little sister basically living with me for no good reason. I make a mental note to give her a hefty raise.

"Well, perhaps you could give her access to a few of the old Kimball files to organize?"

I lean back in my chair. My headache intensifies, like a jackhammer drilling my skull. "Sure, that sounds like a good idea.

"I'm on it." She smiles and turns to leave. "Also, I've emailed you the final documents for the Slayers purchase."

My new plan now is to give Kennedy some

busywork as Krissy suggested, and then afterward I'll take her shopping for new clothes. Terrica has nothing to wear to school, and Kennedy could use a few new things as well.

I'll admit that having her sort the Kimball files is just an excuse to get her close to me. To sell her the story that she is actually working for me. Because if I am being honest, all I really want right now is to fuck her pussy into submission. Fuck those files. That's why I have this goddamn headache. I think my body is actually in some sort of moral conflict with itself.

What a gangster I am.

A Bratva joke.

I usher Kennedy into her new office inside my house, letting her get familiar with the files I will need her to file. It's busywork because the Kimball property has long been sold, and we don't really need all of that old paperwork, but she doesn't know that.

"I'd like to buy Terrica some new clothes," I tell Kennedy. "The clothes she wears to school are not acceptable. They're either too tight or too short."

Kennedy laughs. "Good luck with trying to get her to wear something that is acceptable."

"I have my ways."

That was all I really needed to say to get Kennedy on board with the shopping excursion.

Terrica is still at school, so I figure Kennedy will be able to know her size and help to grab her a few acceptable things.

"You can pick out the outfits. We'll go now."

"Want me to bring the car around, boss?" Nicholai asks.

I grab the Ranger Rover keys from him. "No, Kennedy and I will be going alone."

Her eyes widen at my words, and we walk down the hallway together, entering into the garage.

I have to be alone with this woman. I don't want Nicholai hanging around, listening in on our conversations. I want to get to know her on a personal level because her smart mouth and her determination both intrigue me.

I open her car door, ushering her into the soft leather seat. I walk around and hop inside and start the car. I head off in the direction of the closest shopping center, not really sure how to shop for teenagers. Most of my clothes are hand-selected or custom-made especially for me. This is all new to me, but I'm willing to embrace it just to be closer to Kennedy.

I don't know what this woman is doing to me. It's like she is taking my perfectly structured life and throwing a wrench right in the middle of it, and I'm unable to figure out how to fix any of it. It's as if she is this enigma, and I have to figure her out.

I pull into the West View Shopping Center and park the car. "We can pick you up a few things too," I say casually to her.

Her eyes hit me with a stare I can't read. "For what?"

"What do you mean, for what?"

I am trying to be nice.

"Well, I don't need anything. I'm fine."

"I just thought..."

She turns her nose up. "And what would I have to do for these new clothes?"

"Nothing." I know what she is trying to imply and it is pissing me off. "If you haven't already realized yet, I don't pay for pussy."

She crosses her arms as she gets out of the car. "Sure you don't."

I reach her side of the car. "What are you implying, Kennedy?" I want to hear her say the words. I want to hear what she thinks of me.

"All you want is sex. All you think about is sex. All you do is sell sex in that club of yours. If you buy me clothes and buy my sister clothes, you'll want some sort of compensation. I'm not stupid."

I feel the anger rush through my veins. "You've

been here for weeks now, and have I laid a hand on you? Have I touched one hair on your head?"

"Well, no-"

"So is that what you think of my kindness? That I am doing all of this because I'm so hard up for you?"

I'm full of shit.

That's exactly why I'm doing this.

She loosens her arms, her facade crumbling. "I...well, no...I'm sorry."

"Let's go." I leave her and walk toward the entrance to the mall.

Regardless of the fact that her accusations may be laced in some truth, she pisses me off. Is it inconceivable that I'm just trying to do a nice thing for her and her sister? Gah! I can't even rationalize at this point why I'm still helping her. I really can't. Maybe it wasn't my place to step in. Maybe I wasn't supposed to help her. Perhaps this is my karma for not being in control of my own dick and letting it make decisions for me.

She walks up behind me, tapping my shoulder with her fingers. "Viktor," she starts as I turn around.

I stand, watching her.

"I shouldn't have questioned your intentions. You've been nothing but good to me and my sister since we've gotten here. I'm sorry."

That was a genuine apology. It's rare for me to hear such honesty in my line of work. Is it a mistake to want to kiss her right now? Hope not, because I'm going to.

I pull her close to me, wrapping my arms around her waist. I lean down, letting my lips meet hers. She opens her mouth for me, letting me taste her sweetness, letting me roll my tongue across hers. I can't stop kissing her in the middle of this random parking lot.

I tug her closer, trying to get as close as possible to this woman. To this minx that has all my cylinders firing. She is insanely hot and I can't get enough of her. I've been waiting for this moment for what seems like forever.

I kiss her for a few seconds longer, getting acquainted with her mouth, until the moment she pushes me off her.

"I thought this wasn't about sex?" she asks me with heavy breaths.

What in the damn world was I thinking by kissing her? Proving her damn point. I shouldn't have done that, but God, that kiss. Not going to lie, I've wanted to do that for quite a while now. I run my thumb along my bottom lip.

"It isn't but I couldn't help myself."

She has that look back on her face. The one that says she isn't buying my bullshit.

"Fine...Miss Howard, I won't touch you again until you're begging me for it."

She smiles at that, agreeing to my terms.

"Don't hold your breath," she says.

I scoff at her words. Like she wouldn't be begging me soon. That is one thing I can guarantee. I felt her body melt under mine. She will beg. And it will be a magical night when she finally does. I'll wait.

We shop for the rest of the afternoon, buying mainly for Terrica, but occasionally she lets me purchase things for her too.

And for some odd reason, it makes me happy to do so.

CHAPTER NINE

VIKTOR

AS THE WEEKS GO BY, Kennedy surprises me again. She is extremely smart, and after the first week, she starts taking on more and more tasks that Krissy finds for her. Real ones that grow into even more work. Valuable work. After the first month, she is practically managing a good portion of my real estate holdings. She's a quick learner, a people person, and damn near brilliant. I can see why she was close to getting that business degree.

Once we get into a rhythm, she and her sister soon make themselves at home, and I find myself not making any effort to move her into her own place. Instead, I find myself spending more time in my home office instead of at the strip club where I normally take care of business. I trust Nicholai enough that I know the club is running smoothly and Gary has the pharmacy together. My runners have been doing it so long it is second nature to them.

My favorite part of the day is when Kennedy saunters in, with excitement in her eyes, and she parks her sexy ass on the edge of my desk as she pitches new ideas. At first, I didn't even listen to what she was saying. My eyes were glued to the apex of her thighs where that sweet pussy was, but when she called me out for not listening to her, it was then I realized that her ideas were actually good. Really good.

Terrica has finally seemed to resign herself that she is going to school, fully clothed and that she isn't going to pull the shit she had on her sister anymore. She was pissed when she came home and found out that I had Dottie throw all her clothes away and replaced them with clothes a sixteen-year-old that wasn't trying to be a stripper should be wearing. The fact Kennedy was by my side agreeing with me as I told her made me happier than it should. It was like we were a couple.

I've gotten pissed at myself because of it. These new feelings. I cannot allow myself to become domesticated. I'm not Terrica's father and I'm not Kennedy's new "man". I'm just their temporary benefactor.

I even tried going to the club and fucking one of my girls, but none of them held my interest or could even get my dick's attention. It's actually pretty sad. I'm fucked. Luckily, I seem to be the only one who knows it.

Dottie walks in wringing her hands in worry. Her state of mind alerts me immediately. Kennedy walks in right behind Dottie, but when she notices the worry on Dottie's face she puts her hand on her shoulder. "Are you ok?"

Dottie pats Kennedy's hand and gave her a tight smile. Dottie has taken to Kennedy, and the bond between them is apparent.

"Yes, I just need to talk to Viktor. He has a visitor."

"Oh, I'll just leave you." Kennedy's eyes seek mine, and when they connect I see the fear in them.

The short time she has been here, things have been going nicely. I'm sure she has convinced herself that the mob part of my life is minuscule, but this visit will serve as a good reminder for her to know that I'm not the good guy.

"I'll talk to you later."

Kennedy nods and walks back to her office, closing the door behind her.

"Officer Sampson is here to see you," Dottie says once Kennedy is securely out of earshot.

My gut clenches. Officer Sampson is on my payroll, and he only comes by when bad things are happening.

When I took over the business, Officer Sampson came by to threaten me. He had been close to getting Boris thrown in jail for drug trafficking. I was next on the list. When he realized it was my intention of getting the heroin and the meth out of the city, he sided with me. Now he is on my side and keeps me in the loop on anything that I don't know about.

"What's up, Tony?" I ask after Dottie shuts the door.

"Viktor," he plops his fat ass on the chair, his face looks haggard. "There was another overdose," he says, not bothering to beat around the bush.

"Fuck," I mutter in frustration. "What was it?" My voice is harsh from my clenched jaw.

"Heroin."

"Dammit."

"It was another one of your girls."

The table shakes when my hands slam down on it. Tony doesn't jump. His own face is shrouded in anger as well. We have worked for years to get that shit out and it seems to be back with a vengeance. In my club.

"It was laced with some shit that would kill an elephant. They are targeting you, Viktor. The hospital has noticed an influx of heroin use coming into the ER, but it isn't a coincidence that the laced heroin is taking out your girls. Someone is after you." Tony runs his hands through his thin gray hair.

Anger, like I've never felt, runs through me. Rage pulses over my skin.

"Do you have any leads?" I ask.

Tony has been investigating the drugs coming into the city, and I was hoping he was luckier than I'd been. My guys have come up empty trying to find out who is bringing this shit in my area, and I wanted to do all the legwork I could on my own before I asked for the long arm of the Bratva to get involved.

I have a network of Bratva contacts in New York City, Los Angeles, Chicago, San Diego, San Francisco, Seattle, Detroit and back home in Russia.

But if I get them involved, things will get messier before they get better. Some soldiers may question my ability to lead and try to challenge me. That's why I need to handle this myself. I'll look weak if I don't.

"No, but we're thinking about putting in a plant to try and buy it. Maybe an agent posing as one of your strippers."

"Let me know if you need my help." I sit up straighter. They are obviously targeting my people, but these fuckers were about to feel my wrath. I've been complacent about this whole drug thing, something I couldn't afford to be. It's time I step up.

"That may be a good idea. Let me see what I can do. The coroner hasn't done the autopsy yet. We need to know how long she had been using before they gave her the lethal dose."

"Who was it?" I asked, trying to think of the girls in my clubs. I haven't seen any signs of my girls being strung out, but I also haven't been in the clubs as often because of Kennedy and her distracting pussy that I wasn't getting any of anyway.

"Jamie."

Jamie was one of the newer girls I had hired. I had a weird feeling about her, and I should've listened to my instincts.

"Thanks for coming in and telling me, Tony."

Tony stands and shakes my hand before letting himself out.

"Fuck!" I yell, pulling my Glock 17 out of the waistband of my pants. I want to kill something. I hold the black handle, running the barrel along my temple. The safety is on, the slide uncocked, but just having it in my hands relaxes me.

"Viktor, is everything ok?" Kennedy asks, slipping in the door and closing it behind her.

The anger I have running through me morphs immediately into lust. Her wide eyes survey the gun in my hand.

"No, everything's not okay."

I stalk around my desk as my eyes rake all over her body. Each place I see is where I want to place my tongue, hands, and hard cock... I wasn't picky.

Her chest heaves as I walk toward her. I don't stop until we are toe to toe. Her breasts brush against my button-up shirt with every erratic breath, turning me on in the process. I don't want her to fear me or the gun. I just want her to want me.

"The safety is on. I wouldn't harm you."

"What's wrong?" she stammers, the color of her soft brown eyes drowned out by her pupils.

"Everything," I answer her as my free hand grips

her waist, bringing her whole body in contact with mine.

"Oh."

"You're distracting me." I lean her against the wall, my knee spreading her slim legs apart. The skirt she's wearing inches up above her thighs. I'm glad we bought this one.

"What did I do? I've been minding my business."

"I should be at the club more."

"Then go there."

Her indifference annoys me.

"I don't need your fucking permission," I growl into her skin.

"I'm sorry." The tip of her tongue slips out between her plump lips to wet it.

"I don't believe you," I growl again.

My reaction to her smell and her softness is something I can't keep in. I bring the gun to the tip of her thighs, running the barrel along her warm honey skin. Her head falls back, but she is shrouded in fear. It is hot, watching the Glock disappear up her skirt as I slide the tip along the panel of her panties, softly against her throbbing clit as she gasps. I rub along her, wanting more.

Placing the gun back on my desk, I resume my spot in between her legs with my hand running over her heaving tits. They are too much to bear, rising and falling as she pants under my touch. I palm the swell of her tits and squeeze them together until my thumbs run across her nipples, sending her eyes closed as she moans. I need more. So much fucking more.

I want to know what those huge tits taste like. I wanted to lick her toasty brown nipples and suck on them until she comes for me. Just for me.

Fucking hell.

I know I said I was going to wait for her to beg for it, but can't a man change his mind?

My expert mouth ruthlessly devours her plump wet lips as she cries out. Her breasts feel amazing under my palms but the shirt she is wearing is a fucking nuisance. This motherfucker needs to go ASAP.

Aching with need, my hands grip her white button-down shirt and tear it open, casting the line of pearl buttons scattering about the floor. The only sound in the room is our breaths and the pearls as they dance and drop around our feet.

Tearing my hot lips from hers, my mouth latches onto her nipple as soon as I pull her lacey, sexy as fuck bra down exposing them all flush with heat and desire. She arches back and silently begs with her sinful body for me to suck on her again. I palm her and mash those enormous tits together, kneading my thumbs across her wet nipples until she looks into my eyes and then I bend my head down just enough, still holding her gaze as I flick my tongue across her, then lean in and suck hard.

She cries out.

I pinch her taut nipple until she moans under me, then lap at her, reveling at how she squirms in delight--so pleasured by me and yet tortured by the need to come.

"I'm gonna eat this pussy so good," I taunt.

"Please," she moans so softly. I barely hear it.

"Say it again."

"Please," she begs again.

"Louder."

"Please, Viktor."

There's the begging I was holding out for.

Hastily I move, shoving her legs back to her left shoulder with one hand as I paw at her soaked panties with my right. She is so wet. So fucking wet. Just for me. I toy with her yearning snatch, sliding my thumb under the hem of her lace until I feel her hot skin against me.

Fuck.

She is a dripping honey pot under me. I knew it'd be like this.

Her moan urges me on as I plunge a finger into her tight cunt. Her sweet pussy throbs and tightens around my digit as I pump her slowly and deeply. My hand around her ankles push her pretty legs back further so I can finger fuck her even deeper, hitting the spot that makes her beg for my mercy as I play myself inside of her.

Drawing my fingers slowly out of her I let her taste herself on me, leisurely sliding in and out of her mouth, across the pad of her tongue.

"So sweet, aren't you?"

She hums in total agreement for me.

"Fuck." I place my hand back on her pussy and play with her clit until she writhes for more. I let her ride two of my fingers as she works herself so close to coming.

I take my hand away from her cunt and fist her hair at the nape of her neck, sitting her up close to my mouth.

"You want this dick to make you come, don't you?"

"Mmm, yes."

"Like you mean it," I remind her.

"Yes, Viktor. Please"

My dick pushes against my pants, wanting to be free, so it can replace my finger that is fucking her. Her petite hands rake through my hair as her legs try desperately to crawl up my body and hook me to her. She wants me in the worst way. I can tell she hasn't been fucked good and proper in forever. Maybe never.

"Kennedy, I'm home," Terrica's youthful voice calls out. Blasting into our sex fest like a cold, bitter wind.

"Fuck," I whisper still keeping my finger thrust inside of Kennedy.

She giggles against my neck. I think she likes that there's a little cockblocker waiting downstairs for us. Maybe a little excited by it?

"You're a bad girl," I say as I wiggle my finger and she bites a spot of my skin. My finger starts pushing in and out of her as she sucks on the spot she has just bit. God, when I get her into bed it's going to be epic.

"Viktor, Nicholai is downstairs," Dottie says from the other side of the door. "Should I have him get your bags?"

Shit, that's right. I have a flight to catch.

"I'll be there in a minute," I yell as I withdraw my finger with regret. "We'll finish this another time. Here." I retrieve my suit jacket and wrap it around her. I also retrieve my gun from the desk and tuck it into my waistband.

She eyes me, her cheeks flushed. "Your gun is so big."

"If you think my Glock is big, wait until you see the real one between my legs," I tell her as I suck on the finger that has been inside her before walking out the door.

"I need to shower," she tells me.

"Use this one in my office." I walk her to the bathroom inside my office, complete with a shower.

She doesn't say a word, but she doesn't have to. Her big eyes and pouty lips are enough to know what she's thinking. She wants me to join her, and I wish more than anything I could, but Nicholai is waiting and so is Terrica.

Well, maybe I'll watch for just a second.

I grab her a few toiletries from the cabinets and a towel. She takes them from my hands as I follow behind her. "Wait, are you really coming inside?"

Her question has my blood pumping to my cock now. "Yeah," I breathe out.

And come inside is exactly what I want to do.

"You're really going to stand there and watch me undress?"

I step closer, enclosing us both in the bathroom. "Not like I haven't seen a naked woman before."

She bites her bottom lip. "Yeah, but you've never seen me naked before."

I lean close to her ear. "I have seen, felt and tasted plenty, Kennedy."

"Ok then," she challenges. "But remember, my sister is downstairs."

"I'm just watching."

My dick pulses as she removes her shirt, her velvety skin on display for me. Fuck me. She hesitates before unsnapping her bra, and I move away from the show she's putting on for me and turn the water on for her.

When I turn back around she's naked from the waist up. Her full breasts on display just for me. Her nipples are pebbled hard and poking out, and I lick my lips with the mouthwatering desire to suck each one into my mouth.

"Keep going," I tell her.

She does and I groan as she lowers her panties down her legs. The sight of her nude body is breathtaking. Like a piece of art. Soft skin, large, full breasts, dark zig-zag waves that drape down her shoulders.

She is beautiful.

And yet again my cock presses on the zipper of my slacks. This is my cue to walk out the door. I am sure Nicholai is most likely losing his shit, so I kiss her cheek.

"I'll be home soon."

And I exit the bathroom as quickly as I can.

CHAPTER TEN

VIKTOR

I RETURN HOME two days later in the evening. I stop in front of Kennedy's door as I stretch my neck from side to side. The smell of the club still clings to my clothes, and I need to go shower it off but the knowledge of her on the other side is way more appealing than the hot water. I've missed her and it's only been two days.

Tonight, Tony showed up to the club just as I was trying to sneak out to get back here earlier. He'd come to tell me that he'd gotten approval to get an undercover girl in my club to pose as a stripper to try and find out who is bringing drugs back into my city.

To make it look official, we needed to immediately set up an interview and plant her into the club as one of my girls. He brought her with him tonight, so I had to stay.

My newest undercover employee, Janet, doesn't seem bothered about her newest position and has no problem jumping headfirst into her role. She hadn't been there for even an hour yet before propositioning me. I grind my back teeth together as I glare at Kennedy's door. I passed on Janet's offer. Interestingly enough it seems as if my dick only wants to rise to the occasion for the tiny spit-fire on the other side.

My cock throbs as I remember Kennedy's tight soaked walls clenching my finger. She felt fucking amazing, and I can't wait to get her pussy around my dick. It will happen, it's just a matter of when. A low moan drifts from the other side of the wall, and there is no mistaking that moan. It is the same moan I heard when my mouth was on her nipple and my finger was twisting inside her.

The smile that hits my face is instant. It seems as if she missed me too, and her pussy is just as eager for my cock. Yeah, that shit makes me very happy.

With two hard knuckles, I knock on her door. The moaning abruptly stops on the other side. After a second, the rustling of covers and feet padding on the carpet fill my ears. It shouldn't sound as erotic as it did but I could have blown in my pants just hearing a comforter move.

Kennedy cracks open the door her eyes peering through the crack, a blush painting her cheeks, her hair tousled around her face.

"Hello," I say, smiling from ear to ear like a horny teenager.

"Hi." The suspicious tone in her voice makes my eyebrow hike up.

"Sorry, to bother you, but I couldn't help but hear. I figure I would offer my services. I promise my dick," I grab my hard member for emphasis, "will feel a lot better than your fingers do."

Her eyes lower from mine and she opens the door a little wider, her nipples straining against her white tank.

"I don't know what you're talking about," she hisses, but the breathiness in her voice isn't lost on me.

Instead of responding to her denial, I grab her right hand and pull her toward me. Her eyes track my movements as I suck her fingers into my mouth. The tangy taste of her assault my tongue, and I want more. Her eyes roll back as I clean her fingers of the proof of what she was doing.

"That right there is the best thing I've ever tasted. I want to taste it right from the source."

"What makes you think I would grant you access to the source?"

The side of her lip rises as she challenges me. It's so fucking sexy. It makes my already hard cock even harder. If that was even possible.

"Because you want it just as much as I do." My feet move until I am inside her room and closing the door before registering that I've even moved.

"You think so?" she asks her hands already working on the buttons of my shirt.

"I know so."

Her teeth sink into my nipple, the smile on her lips evident when I groan.

"My turn."

I pick her tiny body up and toss her on the bed. I yank off her soaked panties and throw them somewhere behind me. "Stay here," I order as I switch on the light beside the bed. I want her to see everything that I'm going to do.

My hands circle her ankles as I drag her to the edge of the bed. With her heels on my shoulders, I bury my face in her hot, wet cunt. She coats my tongue on the first swipe, and I want more. My finger thrusts inside her as my tongue circles her pulsing clit. I'm not going to stop until she screams my name and begs me to leave her alone.

Her hips dig into my face trying to get closer to the orgasm I am denying her. When the inside of her thighs begin to tremble, I know she's close, so I suck her clit into my mouth.

Running my nose along her seam, she grinds her pussy against me. She is ready to come as her cries grow louder. It only eggs me on. "That's right, come on my face," I say, lifting my face to catch a glimpse of her.

Her eyes squeeze shut, and her mouth opens wide as her hands clench her own hair. I dive back into her pussy, tongue first, and I finish her off as she screams my name over and over.

"Viktor! Viktor!"

I stand up, proud of myself for lighting her off like a firecracker. So, hot. So, fucking hot.

She gets on her knees, as she licks her plush lips, making me want them desperately around my dick. Fuck, I am so hard. I palm my thick rod in my hand, pumping it slowly as she crawls closer to me.

"I want to suck on you."

Sweet Jesus. I can't wait. Just like a lollipop. She

purrs like a kitten, a sexy as fuck minx, as she breathes softly against my raging hard-on. Her tiny fingers wrap around me, replacing my own hand.

I growl as her lips cover the tip. She swirls her tongue in the most heavenly of circles as I fist a hand in her wavy, brown hair. Her eyes glitter with lust. A lust I'm sure mirrors my own. A lust I am becoming all too well aware of.

I rock into her hungry mouth, as I fuck her face. She sucks greedily, her tongue twirling the tip on each turn. She's enjoying this immensely, but not as much as I am.

When I'm ready to come, I pull her from me and bring her to her feet. Her mouth lands on mine and attacks it. I kiss her back letting her taste her own juices still on my tongue. She moans as I grab her ass and bring her back to the bed.

I tear the condom packet I keep in my pocket and roll it on in fast forward. I need to be inside her. Waiting is not an option. Her legs wrap around me and I thrust into her.

She cries out as I push in until my balls bounce off her ass. Her pussy clenches around my thick shaft. It's like my dick is in a vice grip. She's no virgin but pretty damn close to it.

"Fuck, baby, you're tight." I clench my teeth as I try to stop myself from coming right there.

I slow things down so she can adjust to my size. I am being so greedy that it never dawned on me that I'd need to take it easy at first.

"Oh God, fuck me," she begs as she adjusts to my fat cock.

Her eyes open after a while and lust has replaced the shock of my dick stretching her to the max. I take my time pulling out until just the tip is inside and then I pushed it back in. After a couple of deep thrusts, she starts pushing back into me, slamming my dick harder into her.

"Fuck me good," she whispers before pulling my head down and kissing me. Her teeth nip my lip as my tongue assaults hers.

"That I can do, baby."

I grab her legs and flip her over. My hand smacks her ass as she cries out, her pussy quivering around my cock showing me how much she likes it. My thumb pushes against her puckered hole putting a small amount of pressure on it as I fuck her. I look down and see my dick coated in her juices and it urges me to fuck her even harder. Way harder.

Her arms collapse and her teeth sink into a pillow as her fists clench the blanket under her. Her muffled scream and the way her pussy is milking my dick shows me she has finally been granted the orgasm I have been denying her.

The feeling of her tight cunt pulsing around me is too much. Hot ribbons of come shoot out of my dick trying to push past the latex barrier I have it wrapped in.

Kennedy's glistening body collapses fully on the bed and I pull her toward me. After disposing of the condom, I tuck us in the covers and hold her.

"That was amazing," she pants.

"That was just the beginning," I tell her, rolling over to retrieve the ribbon of condoms I have bought just for tonight.

I roll back over to her side of the bed.

"You have the look of pure evil written across your face," she says to me.

She's right. I'm up to no good.

"So, what exactly wouldn't you mind doing next?"

"I wouldn't mind letting you touch me again," she whispers as her hands rest on my shoulders after I slide into the bed next to her again.

"What else?" I ask, pushing her to say she wants to be fucked again because I'm ready to go again and again.

"I wouldn't mind letting you kiss me."

"Kiss you where?" I keep pushing.

"My lips," she says moving in slowly for a kiss.

"Which lips, Kennedy?"

"Both," she says right before her lips land on mine.

I squeeze her ass and pull her flush against me. I can't seem to get enough of her. I lift her up as she wraps her legs around me. I want to see those perfect tits bouncing while she experiences more pleasure than she's ever received before.

Her dazed eyes roam up to my face and I grin mischievously at her before slamming my cock deep inside her, enough to elicit her scream. I love making them scream. She calls my name as I sink in deeper and deeper, in and out.

Lost in the feeling of her hot wetness surrounding me. Her body is tight and oh so fucking sweet, I never want this to end. The sounds of our skin slapping together fill the room, yet I need more. I grab onto her waist to pound into her, harder. Claiming her. Owning her.

"Oh God, I'm so close."

"That's right baby, come all over me."

I thrust deeper throwing one of her legs over my shoulder to get a better angle as her body tightens all around me. Her eyes squeeze shut as she screams out her orgasm. By the sounds of it, I know she is seeing fucking stars. Her body pulsates around me, but I still don't stop.

I'm still being greedy and want more. I am relentless as I continue pumping into her long after she comes down from her high. I feel my balls tighten, I am close.

The moonlight filters through the room as I watch her tits bounce with every thrust. I grab onto one, rolling the nipple between my fingers. She moans, I groan and before I know it I am fucking coming deep inside her. It is some next level shit. My orgasm is never-ending as my dick throbs uncontrollably.

The minute I have function over my body I fling onto my back on the bed, gasping, while I stare up to the ceiling.

"Holy hell, that was amazing," she says, breathing heavily.

It sure as fuck was.

CHAPTER ELEVEN

VIKTOR

AS KENNEDY SCRAMBLES some eggs and throws some bread in the toaster, I focus in on her ass the whole time. Hey, I like to appreciate the view like any red-blooded male, but hers is better because I know I've had it in my hands. I've spanked it, bit it, squeezed it, and claimed it. It's mine, and watching her float through the kitchen lifts my mood.

"Hope you're hungry," she calls out to my filthy mind.

One-track mind, stay focused, I say to myself. Don't let her beautiful ass deter you from your mission. I need to head to the club and prevent any more girls from dying.

Of course, anything I say to myself just doesn't work when she leans into the oven to pull out a tray of cinnamon rolls. They smell delicious. Just like her pussy. Her heart-shaped ass calls to me, and I move from the stool and smack it.

"Oww, what was that for?" She's smiling, so I know I didn't smack her too hard. Although I wanted to.

"It was there and," I shrug, "in need of manhandling."

She swats a kitchen towel at me, and I side-step it.

"What if Terrica walked in?"

Oh, that's right. Our new relationship is supposed to be a secret.

"I'm sure she's seen worse."

"Well, I hope not."

"You might be a little naive when it comes to teenagers, Kennedy. Not sure how, but you are. At least with this one."

"I prefer the term optimistic. Hey, can I ask you a personal question?" she asks me.

"You can ask me anything, Krasotka."

"What is a Krasotka?"

"A beautiful woman."

"Thank you." She blushes. "So uh, how did you get into the mob?"

"Does what I do bother you?"

"I didn't say that. I mean you have real businesses. Apartment buildings, the club..."

"And the pharmacy."

It's time we talk about the elephant in the room.

"You call it that but–"

"It is a pharmacy for people who need pharmaceutical drugs at discount prices without the red tape. You know that the big pharmaceutical companies are the true drug dealers in this country don't you, Kennedy?"

"I know but still, it's illegal."

"I'm providing a service."

"However you need to spin it. So tell me, how did you get here?"

I think back. How did I get to this point in my life. My career.

"Probably at the moment I met Boris Ivanov. He was notorious, brutal, and the closest thing to a father I have ever known. Working for him was exhilarating."

I tell her about the story of when I left Chicago

as a kid, took a bus to Texas, met Nicholai, and worked take-out at some small dive restaurant.

"The restaurant only hired me because Nicholai told them I was his cousin. We are both Russian so what do they know right? He and I worked long hours. We were tired, trying to stand on our own two feet. It was brutal. We were working back to back night shifts, with no money to eat, and living in squalor as we strove to work harder and harder. It was in these dark moments that I realized, that you can work a hard life forever and never get anywhere. That working smarter was the key. That maybe this world is made for the cheaters and thieves. So that's what we became."

"So you just asked the mob for a job?"

"No," I chuckle. "We sort of fell into it. We started small, pickpocketing, small scores. Nothing too big. Until the night we met Boris."

"I've heard nothing but scary stories about him."

"They were probably all true. He was intimidating, and scary with his bushy brows and dark, sinister eyes. He didn't give Nicholai and I a chance in hell to offer our apology for conducting business on his 'turf'. He came at us, offered us a deal and we were too young and stupid to not accept.

"We were now the property of him, and we had

no clue what we were in for. Boris took us from our tattered home and brought us to his place. A giant home filled with other rough boys, some younger than Nicholai and I."

"Wow," she says as she places a large plate of breakfast in front of me. "That's intense."

"At first Nicholai and I kept to ourselves, unsure of our impending future. We mainly did grunt work, cleaning and doing constructional work for a small development of warehouses Boris had purchased in the heart of downtown Houston. We didn't mind the work. Boris kept us fed and well-clothed. He was grooming us, growing his own little army unbeknownst to us. We were blindly following his lead. We had nothing better to do. No other options.

"The men we worked side by side with day in and day out became a brothership. We formed a bond. We laughed over silly jokes and hung out drinking beers on the weekend. Little did I know we were being taken care of by the very type of men I always swore I'd never become. Even criminals have standards.

"Once I finally figured it out, we were both in too deep. Gone was the boy with sandy-blond hair and a hungry belly. I grew into a large, lethal, machine packed with muscles and covered in tattoos.

"Nicholai seemed to quickly fall in line with our new destiny, but not me. I mourned for myself for a time, realizing that I was now part of a life that I would never be able to escape. It wasn't until Boris pulled me aside one day that my point of view changed."

"How so?"

I reflect back on that time...

CHAPTER TWELVE

VIKTOR

Thirteen Years Ago

"SON, I want to show you something," Boris said.

I remember following him into the large space of his office as he perched himself on the edge of his cherry-wood desk.

"This is a family," he stated plainly. I remember his strong eyes daring me to not interrupt and to let him finish. So I stayed quiet. "We take care of our own. We work together, and it's because of this loyalty we remain unscathed to the ways of the outside world."

I stood there, rigid, back straight with both hands clasped tightly behind my back and nodded. Then he grabbed a letter opener resembling a knife and played with it between his fingers.

He said, "There's a way to how this all works, and I'd like to see you become a made man soon."

"A made man?" I questioned.

"Yes...Bratva."

I remember how larger than life he looked stepping closer to the window and overlooking the city. He told me that all of the boys in the house were like his soldiers in training, but that he saw something special in me. That I had great potential. He fed right into my need for validation and for acceptance, and I gobbled it right up.

I cleared my throat. "Thank you, sir."

"Before being inducted I'll need you to carry out a few tasks to test your loyalty."

I stiffened. "I'm very loyal to you." How could I not be? This man had saved Nicholai and I. The life we were leading was heading in one of two directions--jail or the grave.

He laughed a little, his brow deepening. "Yes, I'm sure you are, but this is all rules and initiation procedures. Since we are not blood-related, it will be required."

"I see." I wasn't sure what he was asking of me, but I would do whatever it took to prove my worth to this man.

Boris had a way about himself. Demanding. Domineering. When he entered a room he sucked all the air out and commanded attention. And everyone gave it to him, willingly. Even me.

He could also be nice and kind. Many times he would help the men who worked for him with whatever he could. Especially if they had wives and families. If someone needed extra money for something, he was always there to give, and give and give. He didn't keep a running tab of debt on his workers, because everyone eventually paid him back. He knew they would. Everyone was too afraid not to.

He was also a smart man. One who, it wouldn't be until many years later, was always planning. A grandmaster schemer.

He waved his hand. "Don't worry about any of this tonight, Viktor. I just wanted to make sure this is what you want. There's no turning back."

Those words echoed through my head.

No turning back.

But what did I really have to turn back to? My

life was here now in Texas with Boris, Nicholai, and my new brothers.

When I said yes to Boris, something shifted inside of me. I never looked back on my decision. I wanted to be a made man more than anything. To have the inner secrets and know the inner workings of his organization.

To be Bratva.

Boris smiled when I nodded. He poured us both a glass of his most expensive Scotch from the heavy crystal canister he kept in the highest shelf of his liquor cabinet. He even busted out a few cigars, and we smoked and chatted about my former life and growing up in Chicago. He said he wanted to know everything about me, and I was happy to oblige.

CHAPTER THIRTEEN

VIKTOR

KENNEDY SITS down with her plate of food and her full attention on me. She is hanging onto my every word, and for some reason, I feel comfortable sharing my story.

"From that moment on things changed drastically for me and for Nicholai too. I began my initiation into the Petrov family of the Bratva, with Nicholai by my side. I have never regretted any of it. Life was great. Money, alcohol, women, and respect wherever we went.

"Boris loved how much Nicholai and I enjoyed the life. We were fearless, ruthless, treated as Gods and it became something I craved day in and day out. Boris taught us many things, and after a while, I noticed he would call on me more than any other. We would spend many hours talking in his office. He also started to confide personal shit with me. Shit, he wasn't even telling his underboss."

"Why you?"

"I don't really know that answer. He just saw something in me I guess. It became easy at that point to move up the ranks with him guiding me and Nicholai having my back every step of the way. I was on my way to becoming a made man. I just had one more task to do, and it would be the hardest moment of my life."

Kennedy takes a swig of orange juice and licks her lips. "Wow, what was it?"

Darkness washes over me. Thinking about my beginnings brings up both good and bad memories. I can't believe I just told Kennedy my whole fucking life story. It is a code in the Bratva not to share family business, but I just broke the code. I didn't give her the exact details, but I've told her enough. I told her more about my life after Boris than I've told anyone. Dammit, I sleep with her a couple of times and now I'm in here spilling my heart out to this woman.

It makes me feel weird and...vulnerable, so I grab her hand.

"I shouldn't have told you all of that," I admit to her. "I definitely can't tell you anymore."

Her fingers brush through my hair, and I lean into her touch.

"Then don't," she says sweetly.

I glance back up at her, our eyes crashing into one another.

"You've ruined everything," I whisper.

My hand travels further up her nightshirt to her silky thighs, and I trace over the lace of her soaked panties. Fuck me, she's wet already.

"You're ruining me, Kennedy."

She leans over, our lips meeting, and I open myself to her. Our tongues trace along one another, and I realize that without even knowing it, that I've opened my heart to her. I just laid it right there before her, sliced open, bleeding and wounded, and I pray that she is gentle with it.

I'm in fucking trouble. This was supposed to be a very temporary situation. Now I don't know how I will ever let her go.

We rise from the table and walk back to my bedroom, down the hallway, both of us connected to one another. I slip a finger past the material of her panties and deep into her. She moans into my mouth, and her knee lands on the bed beside me. Removing my finger, I pull her to straddle my lap, and with both hands on her hip, I grind her down onto me.

"Feel that? This is how much I want you. How much you ruin me."

"Viktor," she moans as her body continues to grind against my hardness.

I need this. I need her.

With aggression and deep need, I move Kennedy onto the bed, lying her on her back. I move on top of her and gaze into her hooded eyes.

"You need to move out," I say. Knowing full well I'm talking shit. I don't want her to go anywhere but that's the problem.

She grabs a hold of my face. "I agree ."

I kiss her with all the pain, trust, fear, lust, and any other emotion that is rippling through me causing my skin to burn with heat.

I am rock hard, and there is no stopping me today. The exhaustion I felt from work last night has disappeared, and the only thing my mind can think about is her. Being so deep inside her. Being fused together as one.

My hands fly under her nightshirt, ripping the

lace of her panties to shreds, tossing it across the room. Her eyes widen at my possessiveness which only fuels me on. She sits up, grabbing the hem of her dress, and slowly lifts it over her head.

I growl at the sight of her. She takes my breath away as her tits bounce before me, and I can't take much more.

I quickly drop my pajama pants and boxers. My dick springs forth like an angry bull, and Kennedy licks her lips again when she sees my cock.

This girl.

She really will be the death of me. But, right now I'd rather be dead than never get to experience her like this. I'd rather be dead than never hear her moan my name like she's doing right now.

Her body so ripe and ready for me, makes my cock pulse. I run my dick through her wetness, and she bucks up to grind against me.

"Such a needy girl," I say gruffly.

"Please, Viktor," she begs.

I don't answer her pleas, only sheath my cock with a condom and position myself at her tight entrance.

I push in slowly, ever so carefully, afraid to hurt her. We had a rough session of lovemaking last night.

"Are you ok?" I ask.

Her eyes pop open. "Since when do you care about whether it hurts or not?"

I feel like a dick. I admit I have been consumed by her, by my own lust, and have been selfish. But now I am particularly concerned that it feels perfect for her and not just myself.

"I care a lot," I say. Once again allowing myself to be vulnerable with her.

She smiles and takes my lips with hers.

The moment I'm completely inside her, I stall. Fuck, how on earth does she feel better than the last dozen times I've been inside of her?

The darkness of my past and things I've done washes away, and she is my shining light, keeping me away from the storm brewing deep within my soul. I can't change the past. I will root out the drug dealer in my club. I can at least do that even if I can't be who she deserves.

I roam my hands all over Kennedy's body, pulling, tugging, kneading her delicate skin, memorizing her body. I don't want to ever forget how good she feels. As if I ever could forget. She's captured me. Maybe I'm the one who practically took her from her home, but she has taken me ten times over.

My cock slams inside her as she moans my name

over and over. It's like music to my ears, and I love it more than anything.

There's meaning behind her touches, and I want to study it for the rest of my life. To understand everything she's telling me every time she places her hands on me. My body climbs as I keep pushing deeper inside her, claiming every inch of her. She's mine. And today, I won't let her forget it.

I slant my lips over hers, kissing her with no mercy. I kiss her until we both gasp for breath from each other. I kiss her to let her know she's the only one I've ever wanted to kiss like this.

My gaze drops to her round, perfect breasts and I lean down to take one of her large nipples into my mouth. I gently bite down, applying more pressure the longer I suck on her. I do this not to hurt her but because I know she likes it.

Our bodies climb together now, her moans growing to high-pitched screams as I ravage her body harder and faster.

She begs me not to stop, she begs me to keep going. And more than anything she begs me to never let her go. And more than anything I want to keep these promises to her. To be the man she needs and to never let her go, but even though today I am everything she needs, I can never be the man she wants.

Grappling with this realization, I drive into her pussy deeper than before and her nails rake down my back. It turns me into something wilder, more crazy with lust, and I pound harder. Our bodies are both so close, and I want more than anything to bring her to where she needs to be. To her most ultimate pleasure. For today she is mine and I will exude my power over her, again and again, knowing that she will match me stroke for stroke.

I give and she takes. I push and she pulls. Together in perfect harmony. A symphony of bodies mingling together at this moment forever.

If one can ever believe in repeating moments, or warping time...let them warp this morning to replay over and again for the rest of my life.

I run my finger over her clit, and she moans a long, low moan. "Viktor, I'm so close."

"I know, baby, give it to me. Give me yourself."

Her eyes slam into mine, and our hearts beat together, in tune and in sync as we keep rocking into each other.

Tangled together, we reach that precipice, and she's the first to let loose, tumbling down around me.

"Don't ever forget me," I whisper against her cries of passion, speaking only for her heart to hear.

My body plunges full speed ahead, and I lose control, thrusting, pounding, and tearing through her like a desperate runaway train.

"Never," she replies.

Later in the day, once we are sure that Terrica is out of the house, Kennedy and I enjoy a skinny dip in the hot tub. I've been fucking her for weeks since I got my first taste of her sweet body, and I thought the hot tub would soothe her aching pussy before I bury myself in her again tonight. See, I'm getting better at this thoughtful shit.

I pull her close to my body, enjoying the feel of her skin against mine. She wraps her arms around my neck.

"I think Terrica's hiding something from me," Kennedy says.

"Why?" I ask my dick going immediately limp at the change of subject.

"I don't know she's been acting strange."

"Don't all teenagers act strange?"

"Stranger than that."

I cock my eyebrow so she would explain.

"She hasn't argued with me about the clothes she's been wearing. She actually looks like a nice young lady. She's even been studying on her own. In fact, she hasn't argued with me at all in a couple of weeks."

"That's bad?"

"Yes."

"Do you want me to talk to her, Krasotka?" I ask, grabbing her and yanking her to my lap.

"Would you?" She leans her head into the crook of my neck and I like the feel of it. "She seems to listen to you."

"Of course I will. Anything for you. Plus I kind of like the kid."

"And I like you," she purrs into the side of my neck.

Loving the feel of her body against mine, it is crystal clear that this is becoming more than just fucking. I am beginning to care for this girl. The first time she stormed into the club I knew she was special. I instantly knew that her problems were going to be taken care of by me. That she was mine and nobody was going to fuck with her. Ever.

"Viktor, you have a visitor." Dottie comes outside and smiles when she sees Kennedy snuggled on my chest. Kennedy's body stills for a second realizing that we've just been outed, but she doesn't move away from me. She stays in my embrace and that makes me happy.

"You can send him out here," I tell Dottie, not wanting to let go of Kennedy just yet. Especially when her pussy is so close to my dick.

"Sit down further in the water so he can't see anything," I tell her.

But Tony's grim face kills my slow-building erection.

"Viktor." Tony nods his head, and I move Kennedy behind me because even her bare shoulders are only for my viewing pleasure. Why the fuck did I tell Dottie to send him out to me? Why the fuck is he even here?

"I need you to come down to the club with me," he says.

"Can it wait?"

"I'm afraid not."

"Give me a minute."

Dottie takes Tony over to the patio on the other side of the house to wait while I wrap Kennedy in an enormous, plush towel. My hands grab her ass, letting it go with sadness.

"Bye, babe," I tell her smacking her ass and sending her a wink. "I'll wake you up if I don't get home too late."

CHAPTER FOURTEEN

VIKTOR

I WANT to bang my head on the desk, or I want to bang someone else's head on my desk. Tony and our stripper plant sit across from me as the music from the club bounces off the walls. Another girl has died from an overdose, and there are numerous people coming into the ER with drugs in their system. Bad drugs. Supposedly from my club.

"You're bringing Gary in?" I ask, rubbing my forehead.

According to Tony's investigation, it appears that these deaths are being linked to my pharmacist Gary, which means they are linked to me. Everyone knows that Gary is on my payroll. If this shit ends up being true, I will put a bullet in the fucker's head before the police can make a case. He is a great pharmacist, but easily replaceable.

"Yeah, all leads point to him."

"Let me talk to Gary first before you bring him in."

Tony raises an eyebrow. "You have two days. I can't hold the DEA off longer than that."

"Two days? That's the best you can do?"

"That's even pushing it. It can't seem like I'm doing the Bratva any special favors."

"Yet I'm cooperating."

"Don't act like you're clean, Viktor. No one lives like you do without peddling something in this town, and you ain't no oil billionaire."

I slam a paperweight down on the desk. Smashing a pair of earbuds in the process.

"Fine, you can leave now. Shut the door on your way out."

My frustration is getting the best of me. My patience is short. I don't like to show weakness ever, even if I'm angry. What I need is a drink. A stiff one. One that will ease the tension building up inside me.

I hit the intercom button on the phone and ask

one of the girls to bring me up a Scotch single barrel, neat.

I hit the intercom again. "Hey, bring in Richie."

Richie is Gary's assistant and apprentice and happened to be in the club tonight. If Gary is bringing drugs into my town, Richie would know something. And, I would get it out by any means necessary. I'll be downright ugly if I have to.

After the scotch arrives, Richie steps through the doors of my office. His beady eyes bouncing around. He's acting very uneasy.

"Richard," I say as calmly as I can.

"Mr. Petrov, you wanted to see me." His voice shakes and croaks. His eyes bounce around my office nervously.

I rise from my seat, making my way closer to him. Slowly, carefully.

"Tell me everything you know about why my girls are dropping dead from heroin?"

His gray eyes grow wide with fear. I knew the look well. I'd caused that look many times before. Usually, before I ended a man's life. But, I haven't done that in a long while, and while I sometimes miss the finality of it all, these days I'd rather just break kneecaps or fingers.

"I...I...don't know." He fists his ball cap in his hands.

"Sit down." I motion to the chair and he sits like the obedient dog he is. Good boy.

"You work for Gary."

"Yes."

"Which means you work for me."

"Yes."

"And I've been hearing around town that you two are bringing shit into my town." I hover over him as he sits.

"What? No. We'd never do that, Mr. Petrov."

"Let me rephrase. Tell me everything."

I walk to my locked metal cabinet, housing my collection of weapons. Richie's eyes bulge when I open the door. Running my hand over different knives, I choose a nice blade and bring it into the soft light of my office.

"Let's start again. Is Gary making some sort of synthetic shit and selling it to my girls?"

"No, sir."

I slide my hand along the blade admiring the handiwork of the craftsmanship.

"You, sure?" I ask with a sinister grin.

"I bring the drugs from Mexico, the ones you tell me to. I deliver them to Gary," he stammers.

I turn the blade in my hand, admiring the way the light reflects off the metal of the blade.

Spinning around quickly, I get up in his face. "Bringing anything else up from Mexico?" I run the edge of the knife lightly down his jaw as he gulps.

"No, sir."

"What about any of your runners? They bringing anything illegal across the border?"

He shakes his head. Interesting. Someone is fucking with me and I have a feeling this guy knows something he isn't telling me. Who could he be more afraid of than me?

Sweat runs down his temples, his breathing speeds up as I grab his hand. "What hand are you?"

"Excuse me, sir?"

I crack my neck to the side. "What hand do you jerk off with?"

"R..Right," he says as his voice crack.

I grab his left hand and hold it down on the arm of the chair. Spreading his fingers, I bring the blade close to his pinky. "You don't mind if I take this finger for insurance."

"I swear I don't know anything," he cries and my adrenaline pumps through me. He's lying.

I run the tip of the blade along his knuckle.

My phone rings in my pocket, pausing my

actions. I stand upright, reaching my hand into my pants. I know who it is. I gave her a special ringtone.

"Kennedy, bad time. What's up?"

"When are you coming home?" Her voice sounds shaky. Something isn't right.

"Is something wrong?"

"Somebody named Lindsay is here."

I blow out a long breath. "I'm on my way."

I glance over at Richie. "Looks like my girl just saved your finger's life."

I throw my jacket on, calling for Nicholai as I open the door.

"Viktor, what's going on?" he asks.

"Got to deal with some shit at the house. Dottie's not there to handle it. Get this one to talk," I say, pointing in Richie's direction. "He knows something. If anyone can get it out of him, I know you can."

Nicholai's eyes light up. He likes to inflict pain. It's his specialty. I should have brought him in here, to begin with.

I drive like a bat out of hell trying to get to Kennedy before, my ex Lindsay can spread her poison. Lindsay is a pain in my fucking ass. A big one. Which is the main reason why I don't fuck her anymore.

"I will kick your fucking ass if you don't shut the fuck up," Kennedy screams as I walk into the house.

My feet freeze from the dead run they were in when I see Kennedy's hand around Lindsay's throat pushing her against the wall, her eyes bright with fury. It's so fucking hot.

"You're stupid," Lindsay spits out. "You think he has feelings for you? Where the fuck do you think he was tonight? You can't think you're his only piece of ass?" Lindsay's laugh is cut off when Kennedy squeezes her throat tighter.

"You're fucking with the wrong bitch," Kennedy warns.

"Lindsay," I butt in. "Shut the fuck up and get out of my house. Why are you even here?"

I grab Kennedy's wrist. "Let her go, baby. She's not worth it."

"Are you defending this bitch?!"

"No, baby. Think about Terrica."

Kennedy's eye twitches as I watch her visibly come down from the rage she was in.

She finally releases Lindsay with a small shove into the wall, and then I grab Lindsay by the wrist myself and question her. "Why are you in my house?"

She gains her composure and raises a brow. "The cops came to my house. They questioned me about drugs. They said they're investigating everyone close to you." She raises her hand to fix her expensive hairstyle. "They embarrassed me in front of my friends. You need to stop being so messy."

Her pink, glossed lips smack together as she speaks.

"What do you mean close to him? Who the fuck is this bitch, Viktor?"

With frustration, I let go of her. "Just get out, Lindsay. I'll take care of it, but you have to promise never to come over here again."

"Of course, baby. Just making sure that you knew."

I give her the warning to stay away, and she always agrees, but I know she won't abide by it. Her visits have been a regular thing since we broke up. Begging for money is usually the main reason she comes by and tortures me with her presence. I should have expected something like this would happen. Of course, Kennedy was never supposed to be living here this long.

Her eyes flit over to Kennedy's as she walks toward the door sashaying her hips from side to side. "Sorry to bother you and your new slut of the month."

Once she leaves my house, I breathe a sigh of

relief until I see the look on Kennedy's face. It's a look that scares me more than anything ever has before.

"I'm sorry about that."

"Whatever...I want to move out."

"You can't believe anything that cunt may have said."

"I didn't say I did. I just think it's time for Terrica and me to go."

My stomach rolls over with nausea. The thought of her leaving makes me literally sick.

"Fuck that."

"You can't make me stay."

Yes, the fuck I can but that's not what I want to do. I want her to stay here because she wants to.

"Do you really want to leave?"

"I thought you didn't do girlfriends."

"She was never my girlfriend, Kennedy. We just had a mutually beneficial relationship for a while."

"Like ours."

"No! Not like us. I swear to you."

"The cops seem to know all about her, so she must have been someone pretty special."

"Because she made herself known. You want us to keep things quiet. But if you ever change your mind, then the whole world will know that you're mine. I want to show you off everywhere if you'll let me."

She's still unsure, but I think I'm getting through to her.

"You are special to me, Kennedy. You wouldn't still be here if you weren't."

Since Kennedy and her sister moved in over a month and a half ago, she's been eating properly and her body has filled out nicely. She has soft curves in all the right places. Places I can't get enough of. I wrap both arms around her waist, leaning my head to rest on her forehead.

"I only want you, Krasotka."

"I don't-"

"Only you." I silence her with my mouth.

Our lips meet together into a tantalizing kiss I never want to end. I move her to the bedroom, our bodies never breaking the connection. I need to prove to her that I'm not bullshitting. That she means everything to me.

Once inside the room, I lift her arms above her head, removing her shirt and taking in her red, lace bra. I step back, taking in her beauty. She is breathtaking.

"When did this become so serious?" she asks

sounding genuinely perplexed by our strong connection.

"I don't know when, but it's serious as a motherfucker."

I don't want to talk anymore. I am hard and ready to sink my rock hard dick inside her. Removing our clothes, I fling her onto her back on the bed. With an evil grin, I react by caging her in, my body pressing firmly against hers.

"Kennedy, you're mine." And I mean that shit.

I don't want anyone else, and I don't care who the fuck knows it. I am tired of pretending that this is just casual. It isn't. It never will be. What started as an arrangement, an offer she couldn't refuse has morphed into something else. Something bigger and better. Something I hope that will last as long as it can.

I slip inside her, bringing her to pleasure quicker than I ever have before because it's my one sole mission. Her pleasure. She writhes beneath me, her nails scratching down my back, and screaming my name.

I keep pounding inside her, my body begging for the release I know is coming. The release feels much better when I'm deep inside her.

"Oh God, Viktor," she cries as I relentlessly pick up momentum and every thrust becomes more powerful than the last. She feels so good wrapped around me as I plunge deep into her pussy. If I can only fuck her hard enough, rough enough, maybe for one goddamn minute she'll regret ever saying that she wants to leave.

I fist my hand into her dark curls.

My rhythm picks up, my speed now unmasked. I feel like a fucking beast on fire. She bucks beneath me as I fuck her mouth with my tongue. God, she tastes like cherries and cream.

"Damn, you're so tight," I hiss. Weeks of daily fucking this beautiful woman and she's still tight as a drum.

"Viktor, I'm going to come."

"That's right, baby. Come on my cock."

My own orgasm isn't far away, and I want to hold off a bit longer. I don't ever want to stop fucking this woman.

Her body trembles as the first signs of her orgasm shake her. Through hooded eyes, I lean back a bit to catch the curve of her lip as she moans. Her back arches off the bed and her nails dig so deep into my back, I know she's left marks.

"Fuck yeah," I say, watching her tits bounce with

each thrust. My balls start to tighten. "Shit, I'm going to come."

Her inner walls clench down on my cock as her eyes squeezed shut. "Viktor. Oh, God."

"That's right," I say panting heavily. "Come hard on my dick."

With that, I come crashing down around her. My highs and lows mixing with hers. We are reaching our climax together, and I want to give her everything in this moment.

After we come down from our high, I hold her tight against me. Spooning her sweet body, I run my fingers through her wavy curls.

"I still need you to talk to Terrica," she says after we lay in each other's arms for a while.

"What do you think is wrong?" It is odd that I haven't seen her coming or going lately. "Where's she been?"

"I don't know. But, something isn't right."

I pull her body closer, kissing her on top of her head. "I'll talk to her. I promise. But I'll also have Nicholai look into it."

"Ok."

She wraps her arms tighter around me in a way that makes me feel as if I've truly become a lifeline to her. As if she feels safer when she's with me. It makes me feel good and wanted. It makes me feel powerful.

"Don't worry, baby," I tell her.

Part of me wants to tell her about the drugs in my club, to share some of my worries with her as well, but I don't want to worry her with the deaths. I would hate to cause her any more stress if she doesn't need it. I mean who actually needs it.

No, this is my cross to bear. My club. My problem. I am here to make her life better, not add more drama to it, and that's what the fuck I'm going to do.

CHAPTER FIFTEEN

VIKTOR

IT'S funny when you plan your life. You try to be a better person. You fucking try not to let the darkness take over, but it seeps in anyway.

It was Boris who first showed me the path of destruction. He pulled me aside, placed a gun in my hand and told me to shoot.

I gazed at the man he wanted me to kill. His gray eyes staring back at me. He was afraid, begging for his life with everything he had.

Boris leaned close to my ear and said, "Son, it's survival of the fittest. Either they survive, or we do, now shoot that motherfucker."

And a second, no less than a second, before I pulled the trigger, I glanced in the man's eyes and I saw no fear there. He knew his time had come. In seconds, he had come to terms with it. He had surrendered.

I often think about that. My first kill. How hard it was for me.

Right after I shot him, I ran to the bathroom and puked my guts out. Boris laughed at me for three days.

I have to say, that since that first kill, it has gotten easier.

Now, it's nothing. The feeling, the emotion has been ripped from my chest, and I don't even think about the person in front of the gun. Sometimes it's quick, not a second thought as a gun is pointed at you and you shoot first. Yet, most times it's calculated, meticulous, and planned so carefully that it takes the rush away when you kill in cold-blood.

It changes you in a way that you're never the same again.

Thankfully those days are long behind me, and I have men to do my bidding now. But, if I find out who is bringing dirty drugs into my club, I may just have to resort back to old tactics. I couldn't imagine who would be stupid enough to try to fuck me over.

What were they even thinking? And why the fuck were they trying to get to me? What was their end game?

Since cleaning up the Petrov family branch of the Bratva, I generally play by the rules, for the most part. I do everything by the book, sort of. But, one thing is for certain, whoever it is fucking with me, is as good as dead.

Once Kennedy falls asleep in my arms, I slide out of bed and head to Terrica's room. The door is closed and locked but her light is on.

"You in there, Terrica?"

"Yeah."

"You good?"

"Yeah, just sleepy."

"You dressed?"

"No, I'm in bed."

"With the light on?"

"I'm taking out my contacts. Anything other questions you want to ask?"

"Nah, I'll talk to you in the morning."

"K."

I decide now is not the time to try and have a talk with a snarky teenager, so I head to my office down the hall and finally call Gary. Remarkably, Nicholai didn't get anywhere with his interrogation. So I've only got two days to get to the bottom of it myself by talking to the source.

I tell him to come by the house. We need to talk in person. I won't allow any more people to die in my club. If Gary is the one bringing in the shit drugs, I'll kill the mother fucker. I've done worse for less.

He knows how I feel about smack and meth. How hard I worked to get rid of that shit in my town. He agreed with me that it made business sense to only deal antibiotics and pain pills. Part of me can't really believe that he's the one responsible for this clusterfuck.

Nicholai is waiting outside for him and escorts him inside the house. When he knocks on my office door, I tell him to enter.

"Good evening, sir."

His glasses fall down his nose, and his long finger pushes them back up when he enters. He walks and talks like a frightened little nerd, but I've learned the hard way to never underestimate your opponent. So I don't.

"Ah, Gary, please sit down."

He takes a seat in the leather chair across from me. My large oak desk separates us, and he doesn't appear nervous.

"What do you need at this hour? Is everything okay?" His nasal voice is cool and collected.

"Gary, I'm not going to beat around the bush here. Someone is bringing drugs into my club. Girls are dying. I'm hearing reports that it's you." I steel him with a hard stare, never blinking or breaking eye contact.

Gary squirms in his seat, laughing a bit as he realizes I am serious."

Oh shit, you don't believe them, do you? Who's saying this?"

I press my fingers to the bridge of my nose, trying to ward off the tension rising. I was pissed.

"It isn't important."

"I swear to you, on my daughter, I'm not passing any drugs through your club. Nothing that you don't already know about."

I stare into his eyes for a long while. I want to believe him. I really do. I've known Gary for a long time. Hell, he is the one who helped me take this part of the business to the next level. His honest eyes seek me out, never wavering. "I believe you. But, that still leaves a problem."

"What's that?" he asks, never breaking eye contact.

"Girls are dying. If it's not you then who is it?"

My voice rises on the last word, anger raging through me.

I need to get to the bottom of this and right now.

A few minutes after Gary leaves my office, Nicholai and I are having a whiskey when my office phone rings.

"Hello," I answer, pinching the bridge of my nose, letting the stress roll off my shoulders.

"You need to get down here. Some shit is going down," the cop posing as a stripper in my club says.

I hang up on the plant while she was still blabbing away. "Fuck."

"What is it, boss?"

"Trouble at the club."

Nicholai grabs a set of keys, and we both rush out my front door to the Benz.

"Let's go."

When I enter the club, the bright lights shine against the soft curves of all the dancers on stage. My dancers. A few new girls grace the stage and I shake my head. Nicholai must have hired new girls and not told me.

"What the fuck, Nicholai?" I turn to him. All he does is give me a goofy grin and shrug his shoulders.

The plant, working for me, walks toward us. I don't even want to call her by her name. Her messy hair and slinky dress were a mismatched array of reds and purples. It makes her appear sluttier than I knew she was. She was trying too hard and it made her look like an amateur. Someone I would never hire.

"Come on," I say.

She follows me into my office and I slam the door shut.

"What's going on?" I ask, the tension building between the spot between my shoulder blades.

She makes sure the door is locked, and slowly raises her gaze to meet mine. I shake my head, knowing the game she is playing. Fuck this. It won't work out well for her, but something is going on and I'm betting that she actually knows something even though she's clearly trying to fuck me.

"Mr. Petrov, sit down and relax. I'll tell you everything I've found out. But, first, you need to blow off some steam." She stalks across my office in her trashy get up.

I cross my arms over my chest, not moving from my position in front of my desk. "Why don't you just tell me. I've had a long night, and I would kind of like to get back home."

I wasn't lying, I have a sweet little body waiting

for me in my bed. Maybe if I could make this quick, I could wake Kennedy up and go at it again with her.

Fingers curl around the top button of my shirt. I wrap my hand around her butterfly-tattooed wrist and yank her hand away. Funny how my cock only comes to attention for Kennedy these days. Definitely not for this woman.

"Oh, come on, you need to relax. I have just the thing." She sinks to her knees.

Fuck me. Houston's finest, huh?

I'd be lying if I didn't admit to having a momentary lapse of judgment, almost allowing it to happen. It would be so easy. But, Kennedy's lips come to mind and my cock won't cooperate as the cop starts to unzip my pants with her hands.

I look down at the woman on the floor, her mop of messy hair, ready to suck and shake my head no. This isn't right. I don't want any part of this skank or what she is trying to offer. Before I can tell her to get up though, the door swings open. Shit.

Kennedy storms into the office with tears streaming down her face. "Terrica's in the hos...oh," she says, seeing the brunette between my legs, with my zipper down.

Fuck, me. Fuck, me.

I push away the brunette with a palm to her forehead and start begging.

"Wait, Kennedy, no. It's not what it looks like." I pull my zipper up, stepping around the plant and yanking her by the arm to get up. "Get the fuck out."

She pouts her big, red lips. "No blow job then? Oh, come on, we both know you wanted it." She twirls one finger around her long, knotted hair.

I am absolutely furious with this bitch and with myself. I know this looks bad. The look I give the plant tells her everything I need to say, and she leaves in a rush. Anger consumes me, but anger consumes Kennedy more. She appears as if she wants to kill me, or anyone who crosses her path but I'm grateful that at least she didn't run out. At least she stayed to stand her ground.

"Kennedy, it isn't what you think." I rush over to her, placing my arms atop her shoulders.

"Terrica's in the hospital. I came here to tell you, but I see that your last fuck buddy Lindsay was right." She wriggles free from my grasp and leaves the office. "You're incapable of caring about anything besides your own dick."

I chase after her, running through the dim lights of the back hallway. "Kennedy, wait!"

When I reach her, the tears stop and she whips

her head around. "Leave me alone. I trusted you. You're not who I thought you were. Actually, you're exactly who I knew you were. I'm the dumbass."

"You have to believe me..." Before I can finish she is already shaking her head and turning away from me.

I watch her walk away, my heart pounding in my chest, hating myself more than I ever have. How could I fix this? Because more than anything this needed to be fixed immediately. I wouldn't ruin the best thing I've ever had. The best thing that's ever happened to me for something that wasn't what she thought it was. I need her to believe me. I need her to understand that the feelings that are growing for her in my chest are genuine. I am falling for this woman, and more than anything I need her to know it. I need her to believe it.

I feel like my life is spiraling out of control. A few months ago I had it all. Now, I have a club with girls dying left and right from a very big drug problem, and a police officer planted in my club to catch the fucker but instead, is fucking up my life.

Fuck that shit.

This is not how I am going to let this shit go down.

Should I just say out loud what we're all thinking

at this point? That I might just be in love with Kennedy Howard. That I've gotten used to working with her, living with her, laughing with her, and making love to her. That I don't want it to end. And that I would do anything for her.

I guess I just did.

CHAPTER SIXTEEN

VIKTOR

I MAKE my way to the hospital in a blur, not letting anything that happened tonight deter me from making Kennedy mine once and for all.

Perhaps she can never want me knowing who I truly am and what I do to pay the bills. The choices I've made. The bad man I really am. But I have to try. I know I don't deserve her, but I'm already lost without her. I've got to try.

I try pushing any negative thoughts away as I drive my car, racing toward the hospital. I'm not just chasing after Kennedy, but I truly need to make sure that Terrica is okay. Something happened to her on my watch, and I am actually beginning to care about her as well. Crazy, I know. But, these girls were both wiggling their ways into my heart.

I arrive at the hospital, glancing at the nurses' station off in the distance. After I receive Terrica's room number, I go to the elevator to head upstairs as quickly as possible. I worry about what will be waiting for me when I get up there. Is Terrica okay?

When the elevator doors open, I step into the white tiled hallway, seeing the room I need on my left. Terrica is lying in the bed, an IV sticking into her arm. She appears as if she is sleeping, but when I step inside her eyes open.

I look all around the room but Kennedy isn't around, and I breathe a sigh of relief. I needed to talk to Kennedy, to make her understand, but first I had to think about what to say. I've never been in a relationship before, I don't know what to do. How to fix this.

Terrica tries to smile, and I step closer. Sitting on the chair next to her bed, I grab her chart to see why she is here.

Drug overdose.

"Terrica, what were you thinking?"

She didn't speak, her eyes just watching my every move.

"You're a smart girl. Why are you throwing your life away?"

Tears well in her eyes and she glances at her hands on her lap. "I..I..don't know."

"Are you trying to kill yourself?"

"No."

"You almost did."

"I did?"

"You're being selfish. Your sister loves you. What would she do if you died?"

She begins to cry, and I lean over to squeeze her hand to offer some comfort.

"I'm sorry, Viktor."

"You need to apologize to your sister."

"You might have some apologizing of your own to do. Kennedy seems pretty upset with you too." A small smile appears on her lips.

"You know about us?"

"Of course. We all live in the same house and your walls are not as thick as you think."

I chuckle. "How do you know about our...misunderstanding today?"

"She texted me a few minutes ago."

"Okay so yes, I fucked up. Well, she thinks I

fucked up, but I didn't. I need to explain what really happened to her, but I'm a little stuck for words. I'm not doing a good job of it. I've never felt this way before about anyone. I kind of love her and I don't want to fuck it up any worse than I already have."

It feels good to say it, to finally get the feelings off my chest and out into the open like that. Sure, I'm talking to a teenager about those feelings right now, but that's okay. Baby steps.

"Kind of love her?" Terrica asks.

I smile. "Alright, I do love her. A lot."

The door creaks behind me, and I turn over my shoulder. Kennedy's tear-stained cheeks hide the small smile playing at her lips. I don't know how long she's been standing there, but I'm so relieved to see her.

I jump from the chair. "Kennedy." My arms instinctively wrap around her waist. "I'm so sorry. She tried to seduce me. She's a bitch, and I don't think she's doing any good as a plant for the drugs."

"A plant?"

"She's an undercover cop working a case for me. Nothing was going to happen between us. You walked in just as I was about to tell her to pack her shit and go."

"You kind of love me?" she asks still teary-eyed

"I kind of, sort of, very much fucking love you. Which is unfortunate for you, because that means you're stuck with a Russian Bratva boss for the rest of your natural life."

Our lips smash together, tongues dancing inside each other's mouths. She is perfect for me, and I will never let her go. Good thing she likes me too.

"Ahem, get a room you two," Terrica says from her hospital bed.

Kennedy pulls her mouth from mine and rushes to her sister's bedside. "You scared me. Please don't ever do that again. I already lost mom and dad. I can't lose you too."

I watch the exchange, hoping we can find some help for Terrica together. Then a lightbulb goes off. I wonder if the person bringing the drugs into my club is the same person selling to Terrica.

"Terrica, where did the drugs come from?"

She appears afraid to tell me until Kennedy urges her on. "It's safe in here. Tell us.

Terrica takes a deep breath. "One of the girls at the club."

"Bliss? What made you go to the club?"

"I was told that was the easiest place to score at the cheapest price."

"What did you buy?"

"I thought I was buying cocaine, but I think they sold me heroin."

"Who did you buy it from?"

"I don't know her name. She's new I think. She has colorful hair, really frizzy, and she has a tattoo of a butterfly on her wrist."

That is all I needed to hear. I walk out of the room after saying goodbye to Kennedy and Terrica. With my phone in hand, I dial Tony's number.

"Your cop friend, Janet, is in on it. What the fuck, Tony?"

"Janet has been taken off the case. She's been tampering with the evidence we believe in another case."

News to me.

"Are you kidding? She was at my club tonight."

"Really? I'll give her a call and have her come back down to the station."

"Do that."

Something was very off about this. Who is this cop, why is she dealing in my club, and why was she coming onto me tonight at the club?

I peek back into the room with Terrica and Kennedy. "I'm sorry, but I'll be back in a bit. I have to go deal with Janet."

"Who's she?"

"The undercover cop. That's who sold Terrica the drugs."

"The bitch who was on her knees tonight?"

"The very same."

Kennedy moves to the edge of her chair. "You're going to confront her by yourself?"

"I'll be fine." I closed the distance between us and leaned over to kiss her cheek. "This is what I do."

"Be careful, Mr. Petrov, that woman almost had your dick in her mouth."

"Don't fret, Miss Howard, I will leave that distinct pleasure for only you to enjoy."

"Eww! Would you both cut it out," Terrica complains.

Leaving both of my girls in the hospital room, I head off to the club to end this once and for all. I know she's still there because Nicholai has been keeping an eye on her. She never actually left after the huge blow-up between me, her and Kennedy.

I hop into my black Mercedes and drive as fast as I can to the club. I park in the rear of the lot, trying to be as incognito as possible. The club is dying down, the morning sun not far off in the distance.

Janet exits the bar, her purple dress hiked up her shapely thighs. Her multi-colored hair is shining from under the one lone lamppost.

She gabs into the phone in her hand, as she slings her oversized purse over her shoulder. She waves to the bouncer and hops into her little, red sports car. Driving down a long, city street, I stay a few cars behind her as she turns down yet another unfamiliar road.

Where the fuck is she going?

She pulls into an abandoned warehouse parking lot. It's not quite sunrise, so my car is still hidden well. I step clear of the car and shut the door as quietly as I can.

She enters the warehouse, and I follow her inside. Managing to steer clear of her, I watch as she talks with someone.

The figure looked familiar. Fuck.

It was a woman, it is...Lindsay.

Lindsay and the plant speak in hushed tones, but it is clear what is going down here.

Lindsay wants to ruin me.

Such a spiteful little bitch.

Before I put a bullet in their heads, I need to snoop a little longer. I need to get closer. I move an inch and an old drain pipe whistles through the air as I knock it over. Shit.

"Who's there?" Lindsay calls out.

They both move toward me, and there is no

hiding now. No way not to be seen. Plus I'm Viktor fucking Petrov. I don't hide like a rat in the corner.

I step into the light. "What the fuck is this, Lindsay?"

"Viktor."

Lindsay glares at Janet. "I see someone followed you." Obviously upset I was able to follow her here.

I pull out my Glock but keep it close to the side of my right leg.

"The gig is up, Lindsay. What are you thinking? You are fucking with my livelihood. Innocent girls are dead."

"Skanky druggies are dead. Who cares about them," Lindsay moves closer as the plant leans against a wall to my left. "You certainly never have."

"Have you lost your mind?" I say.

"You don't care about anyone or anything, Viktor. You are cold and empty inside. I wanted you to see what a fuck up you truly are." Lindsay moves closer and I step further away. Her flushed skin giving away the clear anger in her face. She is definitely losing her shit. Maybe I have that effect on women.

No time for jokes, Viktor.

The plant sidesteps, bringing her closer to me as well.

How cute.

They are moving in on me.

Oops, not cute.

My vision blurs as I feel the iron pipe connects with my skull.

Then...blackness.

CHAPTER SEVENTEEN

VIKTOR

MY HANDS WON'T MOVE. My head feels dizzy as I try to open my eyes. Laughter in the distance pulls me further into the situation.

I take in my surroundings. I'm tied to a chair with Lindsay and Janet huddling in a corner of the vast room. I glance around, looking for anything to help aid me in my escape. Nothing. The airy warehouse is dark and dank, and I for the first time I worry that I won't be able to charm my way out of this one. I might actually have to kill these chicks.

I decide to remain quiet, let them talk first. Hear their demands, and then react.

"Ah, someone just woke up," Janet says. "No one turns down this." She holds her dirty pussy like a man would grab his dick.

"Classy," I deadpan.

"Calm down," Lindsay says to Janet, moving around her to stand in front of me. "Now what to do with you, big bad, Bratva boss," she cackles.

Her voice makes my head throb, punishing me for being here. How did I allow two lunatics to get me into this position? I should be home, with Kennedy. I should be anywhere but here. This is embarrassing. Somewhere in heaven or hell, Boris is laughing at me.

Wrestling with the ties on my hands, I try to break free. "What do you want? What's your endgame here?"

Lindsay walks around me, her long legs taking each step slowly. "I want the club, I want the company, I want everything."

"That's never going to happen," I scoff.

"You're not really in any position to deny me." Her tongue clicks against the roof of her mouth as her eyes narrow on me.

"I am. I may have cleaned up a few things, but my business is still Bratva. The thousands of Russians who are part of this syndicate will have something to say about just handing it over to some random cunt."

Lindsay throws a half-empty can of beer across the room in anger.

"I'm going to get you thrown in jail for drugs then, and Gary will go down for distribution." She laughs happily with herself.

"Did you fuck Gary?" I ask with amusement.

"Shut up."

She turns from me, calling Janet over as they huddle in their little corner again. I wonder what they're talking about. I wonder if they're lovers too. How did these two even hook up, to begin with? Fuck it, I don't care.

Out of the corner of my eye, I think I see Kennedy's curls in the distance but this bump on my head could have me complete hallucinating. I focus my eyes, and there she is. It's her! On her knees, behind a pillar. I'm happy to see her, but I'm also angry. I don't want her in any danger.

"Kennedy," I whisper to her. "What the fuck?"

"Viktor, I followed you from the hospital," she whispers. "Then I got scared when you didn't come out. So, I came in here looking for you. Is that Lindsay I see over there?"

"Yeah, get my hands. We'll talk about this later," I say as she unties my hands, freeing me.

I rise from the seat, and we turn to rush out. Normally I would have shot these two and watched them dropped to the ground, but I don't have my gun on me. The dirty cop must have taken it.

"Stop right there, baby," Lindsay says, the sound of a gun cocking echoing through the warehouse.

Kennedy and I freeze in our spots. Turning around to stare into the barrel of a Glock 17.

My Glock 17.

We both raise our hands as Lindsay and Janet come to stand in front of us. At this very moment, I don't care if I die. I just want to protect Kennedy. It's all I want. It's what I promise to spend my life doing if we get out of this shit alive.

Flashing blue and red lights bounce off the walls as the familiar sound of Houston police sirens echo all around.

"Oh, and I called the cops," Kennedy says with a smirk.

"Bitch!" Lindsay screams as cops rush in from different angles of the warehouse.

They yell for everyone to freeze, and we all raise our hands.

Lindsay drops the gun as the cops handcuff her

hands behind her back. Janet is arrested as well and cries like a little bitch when the arresting officer slaps the cuffs on her.

I grab Kennedy and smash my lips to hers. "Don't do that shit again," I say as soon as we break the kiss. "You're crazy."

"For you yes." Her smile is my undoing and I tug her closer.

"Promise me you'll never do that again."

"What? I just saved your life." She places a hand on her hip as her eyes met mine. "You should at least raise my salary."

"How about I give you a really big bonus when we get home?"

"That'll work too," she giggles.

Later when I have Kennedy home and tucked tightly in my arms, I kiss the top of her head. "I love you, Kennedy. Don't ever leave. Marry me."

The words are easy to say, easier than I thought they'd be.

"I love you, too." She smiles and my heart beats faster. "And I'm not going anywhere. You've just made me the ultimate offer I could never refuse."

EPILOGUE

KENNEDY

IT'S BEEN over a year since Viktor and I encountered those crazies in the warehouse. I love how our legal system works. She and Janet are still in jail awaiting their sentencing. It's going to be a long road for them.

To say my life has turned upside down since the day I barged in club Bliss, and Viktor knocked on my door, is an understatement. I'm totally happy now. Totally in love.

Terrica graduated high school, has gotten accepted to three colleges, and hasn't touched drugs again. According to her, it was just a momentary lapse in judgment because of the stress of our situation. So I choose to trust that.

Viktor still runs his Bratva "pharmaceutical" business, manages his real estate holdings, and he still owns the strip club, but he leaves Nicholai to run the day-to-day operations of most of it. Don't get me wrong, I'm not a hundred percent comfortable with how he chooses to make his money, but the ugliness of his business gets easier to deal with as time goes on.

Why? Because I love him. I love that he takes such good care of me and Terrica. I love that he's funny, smart, strong and a survivor. I love him even with all of his imperfections. I especially love who he is when it's just us. His soft gentleness, his kisses, the way he touches me with care. That's enough for me. I mean who is perfect in this world?

"*Krasotka*, are you in here?"

"I'm in the bedroom, baby."

I'll admit it, I am hot and ready for Viktor. Actually, I'm always ready for him. But, today is a special day.

It's our one-year wedding anniversary.

Tomorrow we're leaving for a thirteen night cruise to the Mediterranean, but tonight it's just about us in the privacy of our home.

He steps into the room, loosening his power red tie from his neck. When he catches sight of me, he licks his lips.

I'm sprawled out for him, on our King-sized bed, with nothing but black and red lace panties, and a blindfold in my hands. "Would you like me blindfolded?" I ask him coyly.

I can literally see him getting harder as he stands in the doorway. His eyes darken, his lip turning into a thin line as he tries to fight the desire to just slam into me instead of taking things slowly. "You're fucking damn right I do."

I hold up the blindfold, offering it to him.

He steps into the room, slamming the door shut. "On your hands and knees," he orders.

I comply, lying the red blindfold next to me as I turn over.

Viktor unbuttons his shirt, losing it as he stalks closer to the bed. And then he loses his pants and I bite the inside of my mouth in anticipation. I can't wait to have this man inside me. This man I adore.

He grabs the blindfold once he's undressed, and climbs the bed. He wraps the silk around my eyes, and I close them anyway.

Smack.

He smacks my ass and I let out a little yelp of excitement mixed with pleasure.

"I'm going to fuck the hell out of you," he says. "So, just hold on."

I love the way he talks to me. Like he owns me completely. And he does. I am his in every sense of the word.

I lean up on my elbows, pushing my ass into the air for him to smack it one more time. The sting feels good, and I moan long and hard.

He reaches his fingers into the waistband of my panties, pulling them down my legs. "Need to lose these," he says as he rids me of them and flings them across the room. "I don't even know why you wear these little shits."

Then his hand runs down my spine, leaving soft shivers in its wake. He leans down, licking his tongue along the outside of my ass cheek, up the spine of my back, and ending at my neck, digging his teeth in for a quick bite.

My body heats up, so ready for this man. I want him inside me. I need him there, more than anything. I can't take much more of this teasing.

"Viktor," I grit out, "Stop playing."

"So greedy," he says as he gives my ass a good smack. "Don't worry, greedy girl, I've got you."

And he does. With one arm wrapped around me, he saddles up closer to me. He presses his engorged cock at the entrance to my pussy, pushing in slightly. It feels so good. I love the way this man touches me.

He pushes in further, and harder, filling me to the brim with his thickness. He starts to move, delving in deeper as he thrusts his hips against me. His dick is so big, so ready to come deep inside me.

I can't stand it anymore, and dig my nails into the wood of the headboard as he pummels inside me, making me cry out my pleasure. My eyes squeeze shut as he groans my name over and over.

"Yes, I love it!" I cry out, spreading my knees and tilting my ass a little more to fit him all the way in.

"You feel so fucking good," he growls, hammering into me harder than before. "So goddamn good."

Once he's fully adjusted inside of me I start grinding my ass back, meeting each of his thrusts, and forcing him deeper inside me.

With my left hand, I reach between my legs and fondle his balls, milking him just right, letting him know I want him to come deep inside me.

I am so close to coming myself. I moan out his name, wanting more than anything for him to feel as good as I feel right now. My body comes alive with wonder. My pulse is rapidly pumping through my veins. I can feel it everywhere. Making me come alive with just his touch. His touch makes me whole again.

This man saved me from an unknown future. One that was destined to break every part of me. That I am certain of. I know all too well how the world likes to take people in and spit them right back out. And that's what would have happened to me if it had not been for Viktor, helping me, helping my sister, bringing me into his home and making me his. For just loving me completely, and protecting me from myself. It is more than I could ever repay him for. But, by God, I will try every day to show this man how much I love him. How much he means to me.

I let him keep pumping inside me, with one hand gripping the roots of my hair tightly, and the other on my clit, making my body so close to erupting.

"Viktor," I cry in pure ecstasy.

"You're the only woman I ever want," he growls. "Happy fucking anniversary."

He pumps and moves, screwing and fucking, groaning and grunting until I can barely hold on any longer. "Come for me," he says with a deep command. "Now."

He continues stroking in and out of me until my

whole world explodes into a vast array of colors and sounds. It's like a beautiful kaboom of light.

My moans echo through our room, bouncing off every wall. His grunts of passion overtake him, making his beast-like angst into something else entirely. He turns me on most when he loses control. When his body just can't contain his pleasure any longer. He turns me on most when he erupts inside me, groaning my name over and over.

"I'm coming, Krasotka!"

This is the man I get to call mine every night. This is the man that found me in a world that was almost done with me.

He saved every part of me.

He loves every part of me.

And I love him too.

EXTENDED EPILOGUE

VIKTOR

DIDN'T I say I always get what I want? Well, this is no different. I'm head of one of the biggest crime syndicates in Texas. My employees fear me. My right-hand man respects me. The love of my life adores me. And her sister, well her sister is coming around too. Teenagers. There's nothing easy about them.

I have everything going according to plan. Everything just as I wanted it for years. The low-class street drugs are gone, and hopefully, they stay gone. Lindsay is gone right along with them, and if she even thinks about starting trouble again, I'll have her put down like the little bitch she is.

So now I'm left alone to do business as usual.

I hardly go to the strip club anymore, letting Nicholai take over the whole damn operation. He loves that scene, and I like to stay home, hang out with my woman, and show her who's boss. It's a win-win.

Not only am I her boss for work, but also in the bedroom. I love playing with her there. I love having her let me do the things I've been imagining since I met her. And one of those things is having her suck my cock into her tight little mouth.

Having her suck on my dick is like a dream come true. I'd never allow any of the dancers to do it. I didn't want to mix business with pleasure. I'm glad I held off now, because when my girl wraps those pretty lips around my cock, I feel like I've died and gone to heaven. It's perfection. It's special.

"That's it, Krasotka. That shit feels so good."

I slip my dick further down her throat as I fuck her mouth. Oh, she feels so good.

She sucks on me and I take it slow as to not gag her, although I do like the sounds she's making. I thrust into her, holding the base of my cock and with the other hand, I hold the headboard as I pound into her mouth a little more.

Her eyes meet mine and it's a beautiful sight. It's a look of lust and adoration. A look I can't turn away from, so, I keep gazing into her dark eyes as she takes all of me down her throat.

I don't want to come this way.

I want to be deep inside her when I do.

"Oh, you're being such a good girl," I say slipping my dick out of her mouth and moving further down the bed.

I kiss her swollen lips, deep and soft, hard and long, feeling every part of her open up to me.

She deepens the kiss, her body so responsive to my every touch.

I love every part of her body. It's all mine.

"Let me make love to you all night long," I tell her, wanting nothing more than to do just that. I want to fuck her raw tonight. No latex barrier between us. "Do I need a condom?"

She nods her head no, giving me her answer.

Thank, fuck.

Condoms should be illegal when you're married.

So I push my cock at her entrance, pushing in slightly, giving her just a tease. She grips her legs around my ass, wanting me in deeper. "More, Viktor."

"Are you my good little girl?" I ask her.

"Yes, baby."

And then all at once, I slam into her, filling her balls deep. She lets out a high squeal.

I start to move inside her, slow at first and then picking up my pace, faster, harder, deeper. This is how my girl likes to be fucked.

She likes it when I give her what she needs.

And what she needs right now is down and dirty. Rough and hard.

I bear down on her tits, taking one nipple in between my teeth and biting down until she lets out a yelp of pleasure. Then I play with the other nipple, sucking it and running my tongue around it.

Her fingers fly through my hair, pulling and tugging. She loves this. I can tell with how hard she bucks her hips against me.

Her pussy is so wet. Her grip is so tight around my neck. It's like she's afraid if she lets go she'll lose the connection.

I take her lips, crushing my mouth to hers, letting her know it'll never happen. Letting her know she will never lose me.

I love her too much.

So I pound inside her, telling her with my body how much my love is true.

Her body begins to shake, her orgasm hitting her at full force, and I tighten my hold, keeping her close through it all. Letting her know she's safe now. That I will always be here for her. That I will always take care of her.

She is mine now to protect, and I take that job very seriously. I will protect her until the day I die. And I won't ever let anything bad happen to her or her sister.

I love having Kennedy by my side.

I don't remember what my life was like before her.

I never thought I'd fall in love. I never thought I needed love. I never thought anyone like me even deserved love. Yet, here I am, in love with one of the sexiest, feistiest women in Texas. And everyone knows she's mine. No more secrets. Everyone knows not to go near this one because she is mine.

My wife.

My everything.

I come deep inside her, planting my seed deep within her, hoping that one day she'll give me a son to carry on my reign.

A son who I will treat differently than how my

biological father treated me. Invisible. Or how Boris treated me. Like an employee. A son I'll cherish and teach him the importance of running a business that he can be proud of.

Hey, I may not be the most honest criminal around but there's one thing for certain, I protect the people who work for me and I live by a certain code. Maybe my son will make even more changes than I have. Maybe he'll be totally legit and only run legal businesses. I don't know. I just hope that whatever he does will allow him to sleep at night and meet the woman of his dreams like I did.

That's my wish for him.

I stare into the beautiful hooded eyes of my future baby's mama as I keep coming, unable to stop my dick from emptying deep inside her. I kiss her lips, letting this woman know she owns me.

She will always own me.

I think she always has.

~

THANK YOU FOR READING VIKTOR. It is the third novel in the Red Bratva Billionaires Series, and I hope you enjoyed it. **My new military romance, WYATT, is releasing next.**

PLEASE SIGN Up To Be Notified when my next release is live and don't forget to leave a review if you've enjoyed this novel. I appreciate the encouraging words more than you know.

You can also chat with me on Facebook.

Or follow me on Instagram.

ALSO BY COCO MILLER

Big City Billionaires

Faking For Mr. Pope

Virgin Escort For Mr. Vaughn

Pretending for Mr. Parker

Red Bratva Billionaires

MAXIM

SERGEI

VIKTOR

Made in the USA
Middletown, DE
04 November 2023

41976183R00113